"Nothing's going to shift me."

Kate's voice was firm. "I'm staying at the Villa des Anges. And as for my reputation, I shouldn't think it's in the slightest danger. After all, we're cousins."

"That doesn't stop us from becoming as close as we want, Kate." His voice had a purring note in it now, and Kate's skin responded with an unexpected rush of goose pimples. "Perhaps I'd better let you in on a little secret. We could get involved in any way we like. You see, we're not actually related, Cousin Kate. I was adopted."

Kate gaped at him in surprise. "But—you can't be," she spluttered.

"Believe it, Kate." His dark eyes were glinting brightly now. "If you've convinced yourself that you're safe with me because we're cousins—think again."

JOANNA MANSELL finds writing hard work but very addictive. When she's not bashing away at her typewriter, she'd usually got her nose buried in a book. She also loves gardening and daydreaming, two pastimes that go together remarkably well. The ambition of this Essex-born author is to write books that people will enjoy reading.

Books by Joanna Mansell

HARLEQUIN PRESENTS

HARLEQUIN ROMANCE

Don't miss any of our special offers. Write to us at the following address for information on our newest releases.

Harlequin Reader Service
P.O. Box 1397, Buffalo, NY 14240
Canadian address: P.O. Box 603,
Fort Erie, Ont. L2A 5X3

JOANNA MANSELL

devil in paradise

Harlequin Books

TORONTO • NEW YORK • LONDON
AMSTERDAM • PARIS • SYDNEY • HAMBURG
STOCKHOLM • ATHENS • TOKYO • MILAN

Harlequin Presents first edition May 1991
ISBN 0-373-11364-1

Original hardcover edition published in 1990
by Mills & Boon Limited

DEVIL IN PARADISE

CHAPTER ONE

KATE pulled the car over to the side of the road, and then sat back to admire the view. Blue sky, blue sea, small bays with golden sand, gently swaying trees and vividly coloured flowers were spread out in front of her. Best of all, the whole scene was bathed in bright, hot sunshine. Right now, it looked to her exactly like paradise.

'Fantastic,' she murmured to herself. 'Good old Great-Uncle Henry, leaving me a half-share in a villa in the South of France. All I've got to do now is try and find it!'

Kate studied the instructions the solicitor had given her, and then started up the car again. As she headed along the coast she drank in the dreamy views, and itched to get into her bikini so that she could plunge into that marvellously inviting sea.

Eventually, she turned off the main road and headed down a much narrower side road. At the end of it were a pair of very ornate wrought-iron gates, with the name of the villa worked into the scrolled pattern. 'Villa des Anges.' Kate gave a sigh of relief as she said it out loud. This was it, Great-Uncle Henry's villa. And on either side of the gateposts were the tall statues of angels that gave the villa its name.

Kate got out of the car and opened the gates. The statues gazed down at her with rather cynical smiles on their stone faces, and Kate decided that she didn't like them very much.

'Well, you can get rid of them, if you want to,' she reminded herself. 'You *are* the owner.' Then she remembered that only half of the villa was hers. 'All right, you can get rid of one of them,' she told herself with a grin. 'I suppose that, legally speaking, the other one belongs to Cousin Rafe.'

As she said her cousin's name the sun disappeared behind a patch of cloud, and a faint patterning of goose-pimples covered Kate's skin. For just an instant, she was startled; then she grinned to herself again. It was just a silly coincidence, that was all. On the other hand, Kate's mother had always sworn that Rafe was half devil. If that were true, then it was hardly surprising that the sun had vanished when Kate had said his name!

The cloud quickly passed and the sun blazed down again, but Kate kept on thinking about Rafe Clarendon for a few more moments. Cousin Rafe, who was the other main beneficiary in Great-Uncle Henry's will, and who owned the other half of the Villa des Anges. It was several years since she had seen him, and she knew next to nothing about him, except what she had heard through family gossip. Not that there was any shortage of that! According to the latest stories, he had set up in business as an enquiry agent. Kate gave a brief snort. What kind of job was that for a man? Rafe was far too old to be playing at private detectives!

As she got back into the car, though, she pushed all thoughts of him right out of her mind. She had more than enough to occupy her at the moment, without wasting time thinking about Rafe.

She started up the engine, passed through the gates, and then headed down the drive. The grounds of the villa were beautiful, with exotic trees, great splashes of bright blooms, and paths that disappeared off into the undergrowth. It was also wildly overgrown. Obviously, it hadn't been touched since Great-Uncle Henry had died. Kate's brow furrowed thoughtfully. Could she afford to employ a gardener? Then she shook her head a little impatiently. Yes, of course she could! Along with the half-share of the villa, Great-Uncle Henry had left her a great parcel of stocks and shares. Although she definitely hadn't got used to it yet, she could afford just about anything she wanted.

Then she forgot about the money again as the drive swept round a curve, and she found herself looking straight at the villa.

It was great. No, it was better than great. It was *perfect*. White walls and terracotta tiles, shuttered windows fringed with ornate balconies, bougainvillaea trailing over the lower walls, and great tubfuls of carnations outside the front entrance. As Kate got out of the car and walked towards the door, their scent danced in front of her, sweet but not cloying.

She took out the key which the solicitor had given her, and then sucked in a deep breath.

'This is it,' she told herself. 'Your first look inside your inheritance.'

She slid the key into the lock and turned it, but then frowned when the door wouldn't open. The lock wasn't broken; she could hear it clicking back. The door remained annoyingly shut, though.

Her brows drew even tighter together. Why couldn't she get in? Had someone bolted the door from the inside? Why would they do that, though? And *who* would do it?

Then one possible explanation occurred to her. She knew that Great-Uncle Henry had had a housekeeper to look after him during the last couple of years, when his health hadn't been so good. Perhaps she was still here, and kept the door bolted because she was nervous at being in the villa on her own.

There was a bell-pull to one side of the door, and Kate gave it an energetic yank. She could hear it clanging noisily inside the villa, but no one came to open the door.

She stepped back a couple of paces and looked up at the windows. The shutters of one of the rooms on the first floor were open, and she could have sworn she saw a flicker of movement behind the glass. Her eyes narrowed in annoyance. If the housekeeper could see her, why wouldn't the woman let her in?

Kate gave another frustrated yank on the bell-pull, but still got no response. She muttered something very rude under her breath, and was just reaching for it again, determined to ring it until the housekeeper got sick of hearing it and finally let her in, when she heard the sound of the bolt being drawn back.

'About time, too,' she said irritably.

She picked up her shoulder-bag and prepared to march straight into the villa. She was hot and flustered by this time, and dying for a shower and a change of clothes. When the door finally opened, though, the tall figure that appeared in the doorway just stood there, completely blocking the entrance.

Kate's gaze slid over a pair of powerful shoulders, lean hips and well-defined thighs. Then she swallowed hard. Definitely not the housekeeper! Her eyes travelled upwards again, and this time rested on a dark-featured face that was disturbingly familiar, even though she hadn't seen it for several years. Her cousin, Rafe.

His gaze swept over her, and he obviously wasn't in the least pleased to see her. At the same time, he seemed to be assessing every last inch of her, and Kate was infuriated to feel a faint flush of colour spread over her face.

'Well,' he drawled at last, 'you look a lot more—mature—than when we last met, Kate. But what the hell are you doing here?'

Kate somehow gathered her slightly addled wits together. 'I'd have thought that was fairly obvious. When I found out that Great-Uncle Henry had left me a half-share in this villa, I chucked in my job and headed straight out here. I'm going to spend the summer at the villa.'

'I'm afraid that's not possible,' Rafe informed her.

Kate stared at him edgily. Her nerves had already been severely jolted by the discovery that Rafe was apparently in residence at the villa. And now he was telling her that she couldn't stay here.

'What do you mean, not possible?' she demanded.

'Just that,' he replied coolly. 'You can't stay at the villa. You'll have to make other arrangements.'

Kate's temper started to steam. Who did he think he was, telling her what she could or couldn't do? She wished she could just push straight past him and march right into the villa—half of which was legally hers!—but she could see that that would never work. Rafe was a physically impressive man. It would be like trying to barge through a brick wall.

That meant there wasn't much alternative except to try and reason with him. Was it possible to reason with Rafe Clarendon? she wondered. She had no idea.

As far as she knew, no one in her family had ever tried it!

'Look,' she said, making a huge effort to keep her voice fairly calm, 'I'm sorry if I've turned up at an inconvenient time, but I had no idea you'd be here. And you've really got no alternative except to let me in. I've every right to be here. I'm Great-Uncle Henry's joint heir. Half of everything he owned is mine—including this villa.'

'As far as I'm concerned, you can have all of it,' replied Rafe. 'I'm not interested in Great-Uncle Henry's property. Or his money, come to that. But you can't take possession for at least a couple of weeks. It—isn't convenient,' he finished slightly evasively.

Light began to dawn inside Kate's head. Mentally, she kicked herself. She should have realised right from the start what this was all about. After all, she was perfectly familiar with Rafe's reputation. Her mother had certainly remarked on it often enough!

'Oh, I get it,' she said, a grin beginning to spread across her face. 'You've got a gorgeous little blonde— or perhaps even a couple—tucked away upstairs. That's why the shutters were closed and the door bolted in the middle of the afternoon. No wonder you don't want little Cousin Kate hanging around, spoiling your fun. Well, sorry to be a party-pooper, Rafe, but I'm not going to move into some hotel just so you can have the run of the villa to play games with your girlfriends. Don't worry,' she added, 'I'll be perfectly discreet. You'll hardly even know I'm around. I'll just get my bags from the car——'

'You're not staying here, Kate.'

She had already started to head back to her car to collect her luggage, but his blunt statement made her stop dead. And when she swung back to face him, her dark eyes were as fiercely determined as his own.

'Just how do you intend to stop me?' she demanded.

His gaze slid with clear amusement over her slender body. 'I don't think it'll be too difficult,' he pointed out.

'Legally, you don't have a leg to stand on,' came her furious reply.

'I've never worried too much about the legal niceties. And, if it comes down to a question of sheer brute strength, I don't think you're going to be in with much of a chance, Cousin Kate.'

Kate glared at him. 'Are you telling me that you'd physically throw me off this property? Even though I *am* the joint owner?'

'I'm telling you that I don't intend to let you move into the villa.'

There was a note of such utter determination in his voice that Kate very nearly gave up at that point. Then she lifted her head and straightened her shoulders. She was a Clarendon, wasn't she? And Clarendons didn't cave in at the first sign of trouble.

Unfortunately, there was a small flaw in that argument. Rafe was a Clarendon, too, and he seemed equally determined to get his own way.

He was looking at her now with cool composure. 'Are you prepared to be sensible about this?' he enquired.

No, she certainly wasn't! On the other hand, she wasn't going to get anywhere by losing her temper. 'Let's both try and be reasonable,' she said in a conciliatory tone. 'I'm hungry and I'm tired, and I'm definitely not in the mood for any more of this. Just let me in, so I can have something to eat and rest for a couple of hours. Then perhaps we can talk this over, and reach some sort of compromise.'

'I never compromise,' he informed her calmly. Then his eyes gleamed briefly. 'But, on the other hand, I wouldn't want you to think that I'm completely unreasonable. Wait here for a few minutes.'

Before Kate could get out even a brief objection, he went back inside the villa, firmly closing the door behind him and keeping her shut out. Despite her earlier determination to hang on to her temper, another wave of frustration swept over Kate and she thumped on the door several times with her fist. She knew it wouldn't do the slightest good. Rafe wasn't going to have a miraculous change of heart and let her in. It did make her feel slightly better, though, even if it did rather bruise her hand.

She turned away from the door and then paced restlessly up and down, scuffling her feet irritably and scowling at the world in general. A reception like this was about the last thing she had expected. She had been looking forward to a relaxing couple of weeks of sunbathing and sightseeing, before getting down to the business of deciding where she wanted her life to go from here. Not for one moment had she thought that she would end up like this, shut out of the villa by Rafe Clarendon, who clearly believed that possession was nine-tenths of the law.

The front door opened again, and Rafe reappeared. 'Well?' demanded Kate. 'Are you prepared to behave like a rational human being this time?'

'I'm always rational. And reasonable,' Rafe informed her. Then he handed her a sheet of paper.

'What's this?' she said suspiciously.

'The name and address of one of the best hotels in Nice. I've reserved you a room with a balcony and a sea view. You can stay there for as long as you like, and at my expense.'

Kate screwed up the sheet of paper into a ball, and then tossed it away.

'If I'd wanted to stay in a hotel, I'd have made the booking myself!' she told him hotly.

Rafe merely shrugged. 'At least I gave you the choice. What you do now is entirely up to you. Goodbye, Kate.'

And with that, he stepped back and closed the door.

Kate couldn't quite believe that this was happening. She did know one thing, though. That door wasn't going to open again, not even if she spent the rest of the afternoon thumping on it, or screaming at Rafe through it. Boiling inside with anger, she went back to her car and flung herself down on the front seat. What now? she muttered to herself darkly. Just give up, and find some hotel to stay in? Come to think of it, was there any alternative?

She sat there and brooded about the infuriating situation for a long while. It was hunger that finally prompted her into action. It seemed hours since she had last eaten, and she always thought better on a full stomach.

She headed back to the main road, and kept driving until she reached a small café. After demolishing a huge salad that was a delicious mix of tuna and peppers, tomatoes, olives, anchovies, and celery, she ate several chunks of crisp new bread, and finally finished with some fresh fruit.

'Healthy *and* nutritious,' she told herself drily. 'But now it's time to get back to the main question. What to do about Cousin Rafe?'

In the end, she decided that she really only had two choices. She could go slinking off to some hotel, and be thoroughly fed up for the next couple of weeks; or she could make another effort to get into the Villa des Anges.

Kate's mouth curved into a slightly devilish grin that, although she wasn't aware of it, gave her face an uncanny similarity to Rafe's.

'No contest,' she murmured to herself. 'All I've got to do now is figure out how to go about it.'

She had a couple more cups of coffee, and by the time she finally left the café and headed back towards the villa it was almost dusk. When she reached the gates she found them standing wide open. Since she had closed them when she had left, that could only mean one thing. Rafe had gone out for the evening, which meant that the villa was empty.

Kate had counted on that. Since she had thought it highly unlikely that Rafe would spend his evenings on his own when all the attractions of the Côte d'Azur—blondes, brunettes and redheads—were on offer just down the road, she had based her plans around the assumption that he wouldn't be there.

It was dark now, but a rising moon gave enough silvery light for her to see by as she made her way round to the back of the villa. A little anxiously, she glanced up at the windows, and then gave a sigh of relief as she saw that they were unshuttered. A nervous tingle fluttered its way down her spine, and she decided that she had better go ahead with her plan right now, before her nerve began to crack.

She scrabbled around in a nearby flower-bed, and soon found what she wanted. Kate suddenly smiled. She was beginning to look forward to this.

A few seconds later, she neatly lobbed the large stone in her hand through the nearest window. Then, very carefully, she slid her hand through the jagged hole in the glass, unlatched the window and tugged it open.

'I bet most people don't start their holidays with a little breaking and entering,' she murmured to herself. 'But then, most people don't have Rafe Clarendon for a cousin!'

She stared thoughtfully at the open window for a couple more seconds. Then she agilely climbed over the sill, and entered the Villa des Anges.

Kate spent quite a while blundering around in the darkness and knocking herself painfully on hard objects before she finally found the light switch. She rubbed her bruised knees and shins, then she took a look around the room.

It had pale walls, bright rugs scattered over the floor, and the furniture was functional but very comfortable. The chairs had big, fat cushions, and you could have spent an extremely restful night on the sofa. In fact, if the rest of the villa was like this, then it would be very habitable.

She explored a couple more of the rooms on the ground floor, and found them furnished in a similar style. The kitchen had plenty of modern gadgets, and a large fridge-freezer was well-stocked with both fresh and convenience foods.

Kate would have liked to have seen more, but by now she was yawning her head off. She unlocked and unbolted the front door, went out to the car to collect her luggage, and then headed back into the villa. After securing the front door again, she wearily climbed the stairs.

There were several bedrooms on the first floor. She had no idea which one Rafe had taken for his own, but she soon found one which was obviously unused. She slung her luggage inside and then tumbled on to the bed with a sigh of relief. She needed a bath and a change of clothes, but she was suddenly too tired to worry about either.

'I'll just take a short nap first,' she murmured to herself. She snuggled down a little deeper into the quilt which covered the bed, closed her eyes, and almost instantly fell into a deep sleep.

Given half a chance, she would have slept happily on until morning. Long before that, though, she was forced back into consciousness by someone who was shaking her so hard that she woke up to find her teeth fairly rattling.

It was quite a while before she could figure out what was going on. Still groggy with tiredness, and totally disorientated by the strange surroundings and the fact that she was still being shaken vigorously, she thought at first that she was being attacked. Instinctively, she lunged out, hitting something with a satisfying thump and causing someone to give a loud grunt of pain. Then her wrist was seized and pinned back against the pillow. Her eyes flew wide open and at last began to focus, and she found herself staring up into the fierce dark gaze of her cousin.

'What on earth do you think you're doing?' she demanded, her voice sounding horribly shaky.

'I'd have thought that was fairly obvious,' Rafe replied grimly. 'I'm waking you up.'

Although her heart was still thumping away erratically, the actual panic was rapidly beginning to die down as Kate realised that she wasn't under the sort of attack that she had at first supposed.

'It's the middle of the night!' she told him angrily. 'Whatever you've got to say, I'd have thought it could wait until morning.'

'It isn't even midnight yet. And what I've got to say certainly won't wait.'

Kate hauled herself up into a sitting position. She had thought she would feel less vulnerable once she was no longer lying down, but somehow it didn't work out the way she had expected. Rafe was still towering over her, and she felt uncomfortably trapped.

'You were lucky,' he went on in the same dark tone. 'When I saw the broken window, I thought there must be a burglar inside the villa. If I'd run into you in the darkness, I'd probably have knocked you into the middle of next week.'

'Instead, you contented yourself with nearly shaking me to bits!' she snapped back at him. 'Don't you know it's dangerous to wake someone like that? I could have died of fright!'

His gaze swept over her thoughtfully. 'You look strong and healthy enough. Not the type to collapse or get hysterical because of a little shock.'

'*Little* shock?' Kate repeated furiously. 'My legs are still shaking!'

'Not too much, I hope,' remarked Rafe. 'Because you're going to have to use them in a minute.'

'For what?'

'For getting off that bed and walking out of here,' he told her succinctly.

If anyone else had told Kate that they were kicking her out in the middle of the night, she wouldn't have believed them. She was rapidly learning that Rafe always meant exactly what he said, though. All the same, it was still hard to take it in.

'You'd really throw me out?' she said incredulously. 'At this time of night?'

'It isn't *that* late,' Rafe pointed out calmly. 'You won't have any problem finding a hotel.'

But Kate had had just about enough of this. Being woken up in such a savage way, then manhandled and dictated to—she wasn't about to take any more.

'You might not have wanted me here, but now I'm actually in the villa you can't do much about it,' she told him through gritted teeth. 'Now get out of here, Rafe, and let me get back to sleep.' She flopped back on to the pillows. 'You're lucky I don't throw something at you,' she added darkly. 'You certainly deserve it, considering the way you've behaved.'

Rafe wasn't paying the slightest attention, though. Then she realised that he wasn't just ignoring her. He was deftly collecting together her luggage, lifting the heavy cases as easily as if they had been empty.

'What are you doing now?' she demanded. 'Rafe, put those down!'

Rafe picked up the last case, and headed towards the door. As he reached it, he turned his head and shot a dismissive glance at her. 'I'm taking these down to your car. Then I'll be back for you.'

Before she had a chance to object—or, in fact, say anything at all—he had gone. Kate sat huddled on the bed, with a fresh surge of trepidation running through her. What exactly had he meant by that?

She soon found out. In just minutes, Rafe strode back into the bedroom. This time, he didn't say a single word. Instead, he scooped Kate off the bed, slung her over his shoulder in a fireman's lift, and then headed out of the door.

Kate was so stunned that it was several seconds before she even reacted. Although he had threatened once before to physically throw her out, she had never seriously believed that he would go through with it. People just didn't do things like that—at least, *normal* people didn't.

By the time she had got round to thinking that she really ought to do something about this situation, it was rather too late for positive action. In fact, she couldn't even think straight, with her head and arms hanging half-way down Rafe's back. She tried a couple of ineffectual kicks, but they certainly didn't persuade Rafe to put her down. If anything, his grip on her tightened, and she knew by now that he didn't intend to let go of her until he had dumped her outside the front door.

Going down the stairs was pretty uncomfortable. Despite her weight, Rafe took them at some speed, apparently not caring that she was being jolted around all over the place. When they reached the hall below the jolting eased off a bit, and Kate gave a brief sigh of relief. Then she made a more determined effort to wriggle free.

Rafe immediately responded with a brisk slap on her backside. 'Keep still,' he ordered.

Kate was so outraged that she could hardly speak. No one—*no one*—had ever treated her like this before.

To be slapped on the backside like some child who was misbehaving—it was humiliating and degrading!

Then the black fury inside her head cleared a little, and she began to remember something she had learnt at the self-defence classes she had attended some time ago. 'When someone grabs hold of you,' the instructor had told them, 'the first thing you need to do is to make them let go. And the best way to do that is to find some way of hurting them. A sharp jolt of pain will make most people let go for just a few seconds, and that'll give you time to either scream for help or run like hell.'

Kate's eyes gleamed. Perhaps it was time to put all that theory into practice!

Since Rafe was wearing a thin shirt, it was quite easy for her to pinch a small piece of his skin between her thumb and finger. Then, with a small prayer that this would actually work, she suddenly squeezed much harder and, at the same time, gave the pinched piece of skin a sharp twist.

Although Rafe didn't actually yell out loud, she felt his body jerk with the shock. At the same time, he involuntarily let go of her, and Kate slithered to the floor, landing in an untidy tangle of arms and legs.

She quickly gathered herself together, and glared up at Rafe.

'I hope that really hurt!' she snapped at him.

'It did,' he agreed in a tight voice. 'Where did you learn that particular little trick?'

'Never mind that. Just remember that I know half a dozen more just like it, and I'll try every one of them out on you if you start mauling me around again,' she threatened him.

She was astonished to find that he had begun to look almost amused.

'You're turning out to be far more diverting than I had expected,' Rafe commented, ruefully rubbing the sore patch on his back where she had pinched him.

'I didn't come here to provide you with free entertainment,' Kate retorted. 'I came for a holiday, and that's what I intend to have.'

'Maybe you do,' he agreed. 'But not at the Villa des Anges. I might end up black and blue all over, but I still intend to throw you out of here, Kate.'

She wasn't sure that she liked the familiar way in which he used her name. They might be cousins, but the fact remained that they had only met a couple of times in their lives. Yet there was something about the way he said 'Kate' which conjured up impressions of a close and intimate relationship. That definitely made her feel uneasy.

Kate scrambled to her feet; then she glared at Rafe. Not only was he manhandling her, but now he was also starting to *unsettle* her. She didn't like that one little bit, and she drew herself up to her full height— which, unfortunately, still left her several inches shorter than he was—and then poked her finger in his chest.

'I've just about had all I can take,' she informed him hotly. 'You've been rude and brutal, you've dragged me out of bed, and now you're going to throw me out of this villa, even though I've got a perfect right to be here. Well, enough is enough, Rafe Clarendon! Try chucking me out of here tonight, and I'll go straight to the police. Since I'm legally entitled to be here, let's see if the law can sort out this mess for me!'

Rafe didn't seem particularly perturbed by her threat. 'This is a domestic matter. I doubt if the police will be interested in getting involved.'

'Well, I'm willing to give it a try. And if that doesn't work, you're still not going to get rid of me. I'll camp out on the front lawn, if I have to.' Her eyes took on an even brighter sparkle. 'Perhaps the local Press would be interested. "Heiress Locked out of Villa". That would make a good story, don't you reckon?'

And that did finally provoke a response from him. His eyes suddenly took on a dangerous glitter, and his mouth set into a straight line.

'Try anything like that, and you definitely won't like the consequences,' he warned softly.

'Is that a threat?' Kate taunted him. Her knees felt distinctly shaky by this time, but she refused to let her nervousness show on her face or in her voice.

To her surprise, Rafe didn't answer. Instead, he growled something under his breath, and then shot a black look at her.

Kate looked at him with new interest. She sensed a tension in him which hadn't been there before, and she wondered what had caused it. Her threat of publicity? Didn't he want anyone to know that he was here, at the villa?

For the first time, she began to wonder exactly what Rafe *was* doing here. Her original assumption—that he was here with a girlfriend—was obviously wrong. There was no sign of any girl at the villa. As far as she could tell, he was here on his own. Why, though? And why was he so determined to get rid of her?

She frowned heavily. There wasn't much point in asking Rafe any of those questions, because she was quite certain that he wouldn't answer them. She did seem to have a slight advantage at the moment, though, and she decided that she ought to make the most of it.

'Are you still going to throw me out?' she pressed him.

'I certainly ought to,' he muttered. 'Especially after that little stunt you pulled tonight, smashing your way into the villa.'

'Don't exaggerate. I broke one small window, that's all.' She eyed him thoughtfully. His attitude had definitely changed since she had threatened to involve the Press. Was Cousin Rafe up to something shady? Was that why he didn't want her hanging around, and perhaps discovering what he was up to?

Rafe prowled away from her, turned round to fling another black glare in her direction, and then muttered one short and extremely rude comment on the situation.

Kate raised one eyebrow. 'Does that mean I can stay?'

'I suppose so,' he conceded, with grudging reluctance. 'For tonight, at least, since it's getting late.'

'It's nice to be made so welcome!' Then she glanced at her suitcases, which were standing by the front door. 'Since you brought those down, you can carry them back up again. See you in the morning, Rafe.'

With that, she climbed the stairs, and then made her way to the room she had claimed for herself.

She flung herself back on to the bed and closed her eyes, but this time she didn't find it so easy to get to sleep. To put it mildly, it had been a disturbing day—and night! It was the first time in her life that she had been dragged out of bed and slung over someone's shoulder like that. And it was an experience that she wasn't in a hurry to repeat. Dangling half-way down someone's back was definitely very humiliating!

She had no idea what was going to happen in the morning. Another tussle with Rafe, as he tried to throw her out and she dug in her heels, absolutely determined to stay?

Kate gave a grimace. Wouldn't it be easier just to book into a luxury hotel for a couple of weeks, and let Rafe have the villa to himself? Then, when he had finally cleared out, she could move in without any hassle.

She didn't entertain that idea for long, though. Her dark brows drew together in a determined line, and she gave the pillow a hard thump, pretending that it was Rafe Clarendon's handsome but perverse head.

Handsome? she repeated to herself a moment later, a little edgily. Then her mouth relaxed into a grin. Too darned right he was. And there was not much point in trying to pretend she hadn't noticed, because she definitely had. She didn't think it was going to cause any problems, though. After all, she wasn't about to start swooning at his feet every time he made an appearance, absolutely bowled over by those dark eyes and that gorgeous mouth.

She closed her eyes, reminded herself that it would be as well to go on remembering that Rafe Clarendon was an arrogant rat of the first order, and then drifted into a dreamless sleep.

CHAPTER TWO

IN THE morning, Kate woke up to find her room filled with glorious sunshine. She yawned and stretched her limbs; then she got out of bed and pattered over to the window, to take a look outside.

Although it was still early, the sky was a clear, bright blue, and the sea glittered enticingly. Kate decided that breakfast could wait. Before she did anything else, she was going to take a swim.

It took her only minutes to wriggle into a swimsuit, and fish a large towel out of her luggage. Her suitcases were standing just inside the door, and she guessed that Rafe had brought them back up while she had been asleep. Her eyes gleamed brightly. She would lay a pound to a penny that he hadn't liked doing that! It would have been too much like admitting defeat, and she was absolutely certain that that was something Rafe wasn't used to.

As she made her way downstairs, she wondered where Rafe was right now. Still in bed, she decided, since the villa was so quiet. Unless, of course, he made a habit of spending his nights in someone else's bed, instead of his own. Considering all the stories she had heard about him, that seemed a distinct possibility!

Kate let herself out through a door at the rear of the villa. There was a wide terrace here, already drenched in warm sunshine, and a small swimming-pool, but she walked straight past it. She didn't want to be confined to a pool. She was a strong swimmer, and she enjoyed the freedom of the sea.

Once she had crossed the terrace, there was a narrow path that wound through the overgrown garden and led down to the sea. Kate followed it, her view temporarily obscured by the tall bushes that lined the path. Then the bushes fell away again, and she found that the path ended at a small patch of private beach.

Kate dumped her towel on the sand, and then headed straight for the water. Seconds later, she was ploughing her way through its delicious coolness, swimming steadily and strongly, until she finally decided it was time to take a breather. She flipped over on to her back and floated for a while, taking time now to look back towards the shore.

She could see the red roof and white walls of the Villa des Anges, half hidden by palm and olive trees, and tall, thin, dark cypresses. Although there were other villas tucked discreetly away on the hillside, they were some distance away, so there was no possibility of being bothered by intrusive neighbours. That probably suited Rafe right down to the ground, Kate decided. He didn't seem in a very sociable mood right now.

Since she was starting to get hungry, she headed back towards the shore. After leaving the water, she towelled herself dry; then she decided to sit in the sun for a few minutes, to dry her hair before going back to the villa for breakfast. Her hair was thick and dark, and thick black lashes fringed her deep brown eyes. Rafe had the same distinctive colourings, and Kate was aware that people seeing them together might mistake them for brother and sister, instead of cousins.

She sat on the warm sand, and ran her fingers through her tangled curls to help them dry more quickly. Absorbed in what she was doing, she didn't hear the man approaching from behind. It wasn't until a dark shadow fell over her that she turned her head and found herself looking up at Rafe.

'What are you doing here?' she asked with some annoyance. The last thing she needed on this gorgeous morning was someone like Rafe hanging around to spoil it.

'The same thing as you,' replied Rafe, in a surprisingly calm voice, coiling himself down beside her. 'I always take an early swim.'

Kate shot him an irritable glance. Why did he have to sit so close? The beach wasn't *that* small. He could easily have sat a couple of feet away.

Then a small frown crossed her face. Was he doing it on purpose? Deliberately trying to unsettle her? Well, he certainly wasn't succeeding, she told herself sturdily. She could cope with Rafe Clarendon any day, even when he was sitting only inches away and wearing only a small towel wound around his waist.

'Did you sleep well last night?' he asked. Then his eyes gleamed with amusement. 'After I'd gone, of course.'

'I slept very soundly,' Kate replied rather stiffly. 'Although it was certainly no thanks to you. Believe it or not, I'm not used to being hauled out of bed and slung over someone's shoulder in the middle of the night!'

'Oh, I believe it,' Rafe replied. 'From all accounts, you've led a fairly conventional life so far.'

'How do you know that?' she asked, half indignantly and half curiously.

Rafe shrugged. 'I hear snatches of gossip now and then.'

'I thought you didn't have much contact with the rest of the family.'

'It's rather hard to avoid them,' he commented drily. 'There are so many Clarendons that it's almost impossible not to run into one of them now and again.'

'That's true,' agreed Kate. She eyed him thoughtfully. 'They're certainly all very interested in you. Did you know that? And there are some really wild stories going around about your private life.'

'You don't want to believe all you hear,' he replied equably.

'And what about your business life?' she went on. 'Are you *really* a private detective?'

A guarded look suddenly came over his face. 'I run an enquiry agency,' he said in a tone that didn't invite any more comment on the subject.

'Enquiry agent, private detective—they're the same thing, aren't they?' persisted Kate. Then she grinned. 'I bet it really gets the girls going when you tell them what you do!'

'I'm not some romantic figure out of a TV serial,' Rafe growled, with a touch of irritation. 'I do a simple job of work, that's all. Sometimes it's interesting and sometimes it's downright boring. Occasionally, it's even unpleasant. It suits me, though, and I'm good at it, so that's why I stick at it.'

'What kind of cases do you tackle? Anything really exciting?'

'No. Most of it is fairly routine stuff—divorce work, credit enquiries, industrial espionage——'

'Espionage?' squeaked Kate.

'That's just a fancy way of saying that one company is trying to steal another company's secrets. We try and find out who's doing the stealing, and put a stop to it.'

A thoughtful look suddenly crossed Kate's face. 'Are you working on a case right now?' she asked. 'Is that why you're here, in the South of France?'

'No, of course not,' Rafe replied instantly. 'Like you, I'm just taking a few days' holiday.'

But, for some reason, Kate didn't believe him. She could see that she wasn't going to get anywhere by asking more questions, though. He would just clam up, and that would be it. All the same, it might be fun during the next few days to try and find out why he was *really* here.

Provided, of course, that he let her stay. If he kicked her out, she wouldn't be finding out anything at all.

'Have you changed your mind since yesterday?' she challenged him bluntly. 'Are you going to let me stick around for a while?'

He raised his shoulders in a resigned shrug. 'Have I got any choice? I've tried locking you out and physically throwing you out, and neither of them worked. I'd try a few threats, but somehow I don't think they'd have much effect, either.'

'You're right. They wouldn't,' she declared firmly. 'I've made up my mind that I'm going to spend the next few weeks at the Villa des Anges.'

Rafe didn't even try to argue about it with her, and for some reason that made her feel deeply uneasy. She hadn't expected him to give in so easily.

'What are you going to do with yourself while you're here?' he asked casually, a couple of minutes later.

She shrugged. 'All the usual holiday things, I suppose, Swim, go sightseeing, lie around and get a tan. And when I get bored with that, I might try and write a book. It's something I've always wanted to try, and with Great-Uncle Henry's money behind me I can afford to take time off and have a real stab at it.'

'What kind of book?'

'A novel. I want it to be about family relationships, power, sex, money——'

'All in one book?' enquired Rafe, his eyes gleaming with clear amusement.

'It's going to be a blockbuster,' Kate said firmly.

She was rather relieved when Rafe didn't ask any more questions about it. At least he hadn't ridiculed the idea, though. She would have hated it if he had just laughed at it.

Rafe had settled himself back on the sand, and Kate was rather disturbed to find that he had begun to look at her in a distinctly thoughtful way. She felt the hairs prickle on her skin, and she didn't like that. Quite out of the blue, she found herself remembering something that her mother had said about Rafe only recently. 'Even when he was a boy, he was half child and half devil,' her mother had remarked. 'And from what I've heard about him over the years he hasn't changed!'

Kate supposed that his unsettled childhood might have had something to do with the way Rafe had turned out. His parents had been killed in a motorway smash-up when he was eleven, and after that he had gone to live with Great-Uncle Henry. From all accounts, Rafe had had a fairly unorthodox upbringing from then on, since Great-Uncle Henry had had some very original opinions about such things as education, discipline and the general raising of a child.

Rafe's gaze was still closely fixed on her, and Kate felt increasingly edgy. 'Are you going to sit and stare at me all day?' she demanded at last.

'It would be a very pleasant way of passing the time,' commented Rafe. 'You've grown up to be rather gorgeous, Kate. But I was actually thinking that it might not be a good idea for the two of us to stay at the villa at the same time.'

'Why not?' she said.

He gave a relaxed shrug of his shoulders. 'People might talk. The family certainly *will* talk. You don't mind that they might draw the wrong conclusions, once they hear we're both staying under the same roof?'

Kate let out a roar of laughter. 'You're worried about my *reputation*?' she spluttered, through another hiccuping bout of mirth.

'You think that's funny?'

'I think it's funny coming from you! I didn't have you down as the gallant type. In fact, I shouldn't think you've ever worried about anyone's reputation in your life, so why this sudden concern about mine?' Then her giggles died away, and a new comprehension spread across her face. 'Oh, hang on a sec. I think I get it. This is another of your "let's get Kate out of here by fair means or foul" stunts, isn't it? If you can't physically chuck me out, you think you might be able to lever me out of the villa by pretending to be concerned about what people might say. Well, it's not going to work,' she informed him firmly. 'Nothing's going to shift me out of the Villa des Anges. And as for my reputation, I shouldn't think it's in the slightest danger. After all, we're cousins, Rafe,' she reminded him. 'My father is your uncle.'

His dark eyes glinted in a way that she suddenly found disturbing. 'That doesn't stop us from becoming as close as we want, Kate.' His voice had a purring note in it now, and Kate's skin responded with an unexpected rash of goose-pimples, despite the heat of the sun. 'It would all be perfectly legal.'

'Perhaps it *would* be legal, but it certainly wouldn't feel right,' she retorted. 'I'd never want to get involved with someone who was such a close relation. It would be almost like—like . . .'

'Incest?' he suggested softly as her voice stuttered to a halt.

'Since you put it so crudely—yes!'

Rafe's mouth relaxed into a strange smile. Kate had never seen anyone smile quite like that in her entire life, and she shifted uneasily.

'Then perhaps I'd better let you into a little secret,' he told her. 'We could get involved with each other in any way we liked without running into any problems. You see, we're not actually related in any way, Cousin Kate.'

Kate stared at him blankly. 'What do you mean, we're not related?'

'I'm adopted,' Rafe informed her calmly.

Kate gaped at him in total surprise. 'But—you can't be,' she spluttered at last. 'I mean—well—I'd have known . . .'

That smile was back on his mouth again now. Kate wished it would go away. She really didn't like that smile at all.

'Do you know everyone's secrets, Kate?' he challenged her.

'Of course not. But—you're more like a Clarendon than any of us. You've got the Clarendon hair and eyes—you've *got* to be one of the family.'

'Sorry to disappoint you. It's just a freak accident that I happen to have all the right colourings. But I'm definitely not a Clarendon by birth, only by adoption.' He shifted a few inches nearer, and Kate instinctively drew back. 'So, the fact that we're cousins isn't really relevant, is it?'

Kate decided it was time to beat a retreat. She definitely needed time to think this over! Rather hastily she scrambled to her feet.

'I'm—er—I'm going back to the villa,' she told him in a voice that kept breaking into an annoying stutter. 'I want to—to shower and have breakfast.'

'And make a couple of phone calls, to see if I'm telling the truth?' suggested Rafe with a grin. His dark eyes were glinting brightly now. 'Believe it, Kate,' he advised. 'If you've convinced yourself that you're safe with me because we're cousins—think again.'

And with that gentle threat still echoing in her ears, Kate scurried back to the Villa des Anges. 'Villa of the Angels?' she muttered edgily to herself as she crossed the terrace. As far as she could see, there were no angels around here. Just one dark-haired, dark-eyed devil who was *not* going to get the better of her, or succeed in frightening her into leaving!

As soon as Kate stepped into the cool interior of the villa, she headed straight for the phone. If Rafe intended to take a swim, then it would be a while before he returned, which gave her plenty of time to make a private call.

She dialled her home number, and then gave a sigh of relief when she heard her father's familiar voice at the other end.

'Hello, Dad. It's me, Kate.'

'How's the South of France?' he asked. 'Warm and sunny?'

'Blue skies, blue sea and gorgeous views. It's even better than I thought it would be.'

'What's the villa like?'

'It's fine,' she told him. 'Comfortable furnishings, modern plumbing, and its own private patch of beach.'

'You're not lonely there, all on your own?'

'Er—I'm not exactly on my own,' Kate replied cautiously.

There was a brief silence at the other end. 'Who's there with you, Kate?' asked her father at last. 'Or would you rather not tell me?' he added tactfully.

'It's no great secret. And don't worry, it isn't at all the way it sounds. There *is* someone else staying here, but it's only Rafe.'

'Rafe?' Her father sounded rather relieved. 'What's he doing there?'

'Taking a holiday, the same as me—or so he says.' Privately, Kate was beginning to believe that explanation less and less.

'To be honest, Kate, I'm glad you've got someone with you. I didn't really like the idea of you being there on your own. And you'll be safe enough with Rafe. I know the rest of the family like to tell lurid tales about him, but I think most of it's highly exaggerated.'

Kate wasn't so sure about that. There didn't seem any point in making her father unduly anxious, though, by telling him that.

'Perhaps you'd better not tell Mum that Rafe's here,' she suggested. 'She didn't like it when I chucked in my job and came out here to France, and she definitely won't like it if she finds out Rafe's here. You know what she thinks of him!'

'Yes, I do,' agreed her father drily. 'She always believes every scrap of gossip that she hears about him.'

'Talking of Rafe,' Kate went on, after a short pause, 'there's something I wanted to ask you. Rafe told me this morning that he was adopted. Is that right?'

'Rafe actually *told* you that?' asked her father, in a surprised voice.

'Then it's the truth?'

'Yes, it is. Very few people know about it, though.'

'Does Mum know?'

'No, she doesn't. I didn't like keeping it a secret from her, but my brother and his wife wanted people to think that Rafe was theirs, and I had to respect their wishes.'

'How about Great-Uncle Henry?' asked Kate. 'Did he know?'

'Yes, he did.'

'But he obviously still wanted to take Rafe in after his parents were killed,' Kate said thoughtfully. 'And he even made Rafe his joint heir.'

Her father chuckled. 'Henry always said that Rafe might not be a Clarendon by birth, but that he was certainly one by nature! And the two of them got along remarkably well.'

'One eccentric and one devil,' Kate remarked wryly.

'They both seemed to get something out of the relationship,' said her father. 'And living with Henry doesn't seem to have done Rafe any permanent harm. Some children seem to thrive on an unorthodox upbringing. Look, Kate,' went on her father, slightly apologetically, 'you've probably got a dozen more questions, but I've really got to go. I'm already late for work. Perhaps we can talk about this further at some other time?'

'That's OK,' she said. 'You've really told me everything I wanted to know.'

'Do you want a word with your mother before you ring off?'

'No, I don't think so,' she said, a trifle guardedly. Her mother might get on to the subject of Rafe, and Kate didn't want to have to tell her any outright lies. 'I'll give her a ring at the end of the week. Bye, Dad.'

Kate put down the receiver, and then tapped her fingers together thoughtfully. So, Rafe had been telling the truth and he really *wasn't* a Clarendon, except in name. How many more very unexpected things was she going to find out about him during her stay at the Villa des Anges?

She went upstairs, showered, and pulled on a cool cotton dress. Then she made her way down to the kitchen. Although it was still fairly early, the sun was blazing in through the windows, making it stiflingly hot. Kate opened the door to let in some fresh air, and then raised her eyebrows in surprise as three cats stalked in. One was a tabby, and the other two were black with wicked green eyes. All three behaved as if they had a perfect right to be in the villa, and they headed over to the far side of the kitchen, where they set up an imperious meowing.

'Where did you come from?' Kate wondered out loud. 'And what do you want?'

'They want their breakfast,' said a familiar voice from just behind her.

Kate hadn't heard Rafe come into the kitchen, and she jumped violently. 'I wish you wouldn't creep around like that!' she said furiously, her heart still thumping away like mad.

'I don't creep,' Rafe pointed out reasonably. 'I simply walk quietly.'

'It's all part of being a private detective, I suppose! You could hardly sneak around spying on people, if they could hear you coming a mile off.'

Rafe smiled that odd smile of his. 'You sound as if you disapprove of my job.'

'I think it's a really weird way for a grown man to make a living,' she retorted. 'Not that I suppose you care two hoots about my opinion,' she added with a sniff.

'You're right, I don't,' he agreed equably.

One of the black cats let out another piercing meow, briefly distracting both of them.

'Have you been feeding them?' asked Kate.

'There didn't seem much alternative. They keep up that racket until you dump some food in their plates.'

'Do they live at the villa?'

'No. As far as I can make out, they're wild cats. They go around scrounging food wherever they can find it. And since they've found out I'm a soft touch, they keep turning up here fairly regularly.'

Kate would never have described Rafe as a 'soft touch'. Nor would she have thought he was a cat person. Then she changed her mind about that. Cats were self-contained and extremely independent. They came and went as they pleased, and answered to no one except themselves. They were affectionate only when it suited them, and could just as easily flash out a sharp claw, inflicting a painful wound. On that basis,

Kate decided that Rafe and the cats probably had a lot in common!

Rafe took a tin of cat food out of the cupboard, opened it, and emptied it on to a large plate. The cats immediately began to eat quickly and delicately, quiet now that they had got what they wanted.

'Have they got names?' she asked.

'Not as far as I know. Perhaps we just ought to call them One, Two and Three.' He chucked the empty tin of cat food into the bin, and then wandered over until he was standing much closer than Kate found comfortable. 'I'm going out for the day,' he informed her.

'Going anywhere interesting?' Kate asked.

His eyes grew slightly cooler. 'That's none of your business.' Then he looked at her thoughtfully. 'I suppose there's no chance that you'll see sense and be gone by the time I get back?'

His casual suggestion infuriated her. She had as much right to be here as he did, and the sooner he got that into his thick head, the better!

'How many more times are we going to have to go over this?' she demanded. 'I'm getting really sick of telling you that I'm staying.'

Rafe didn't look in the least pleased by her bald statement. Instead of moving away, though, he came even closer. Kate wondered what he had in mind, and her nerves gave an edgy twitch. He simply placed one finger under her chin, though, and looked down at her. 'Then I'll see you later, Cousin Kate. Although I suppose I shouldn't really call you that, should I?' he added thoughtfully. 'We might both look like Clarendons, but you and I know the truth about that now, don't we? From now on, it had better be just plain "Kate".'

No one had ever said her name in quite the way that he said it. Kate wondered if he used that husky undertone on purpose, just to set her nerves jangling.

Rafe smiled at her, as if he knew exactly what thoughts were running confusedly around inside her head. Then he turned away and left the kitchen, and Kate let out a silent sigh of relief.

She heard his car start up a few minutes later, and she went over to the window, just to make sure that he really was leaving. She had expected him to drive something big and flashy, and was surprised when his car turned out to be a small and rather dusty Renault.

Kate didn't begin to relax again until he was completely out of sight. Only then did she realise just how tense she became whenever Rafe Clarendon was around. 'Drat the man,' she muttered irritably under her breath. 'He is *not* going to ruin my holiday!'

She spent the rest of the day exploring the villa and the grounds, and sunbathing. There would be plenty of time later for sightseeing. The two black cats had disappeared almost as soon as they had finished eating, but the tabby followed her around for much of the day. When she stretched out on the terrace to sunbathe, he curled up in the shade of the sun-lounger. Then he wandered around the grounds with her as she strolled along the overgrown paths. When she tried to stroke him, though, he quickly stepped back with a sudden wild gleam in his eyes.

'You don't want to get too close? Perhaps you don't trust people? Wise cat,' she told him. 'People can be horribly unpredictable. They hardly ever do what you expect them to.'

Evening began to set in, and Rafe still hadn't returned. Kate sat outside for a while, enjoying the brief period of dusk, but once full darkness set in she went back inside the villa. She wandered through the empty rooms, and eventually admitted to herself that it was just a trifle unnerving, being in this big place on her own.

She tried to read for a while, but couldn't concentrate. Finally, she decided to turn in and have an early night. All three cats had turned up for a late supper, but they had disappeared again straight afterwards, leaving Kate completely on her own.

Although she hadn't expected to, she went to sleep fairly quickly. She was woken up some time later, though, by the sound of a car. She turned on the lamp beside her bed, and then squinted at her watch. Nearly two o'clock—obviously, like the cats, Rafe liked to spend much of the night out on the tiles!

Knowing that he was back made her feel unexpectedly better, though, and she relaxed and promptly went back to sleep.

She woke up to find the room filled with bright sunshine. Since she didn't want to waste one moment of such a glorious morning, she decided to take another early swim. It took her only minutes to get ready, and then she headed down to the beach.

The sea looked just as inviting as it had done yesterday, and she spent the next half-hour alternately swimming strongly, enjoying the feel of her muscles exerting themselves to their limit, and then floating, letting the water take her weight as she totally relaxed.

She ended up much further out to sea than she had meant to go. Since she was well aware that it was dangerous to swim so far out when there was no one around to lend a hand if she suddenly got into trouble, she headed back to the beach at a fairly fast pace. When she reached it, she flopped down on to the sand, slightly out of breath, but feeling exhilarated and refreshed.

'You might be a good swimmer, but in future stick closer to the shore,' instructed a very familiar voice.

Kate opened her eyes and glared irritably up at Rafe. He was doing it again, creeping up on her when she wasn't expecting it!

'I wasn't in any difficulty,' she said crossly.

'No, you weren't,' he agreed. 'But if you had been, who do you think would have been around to haul you out?'

'I dare say *you* would have been,' she retorted. 'After all, you seem to spend most of your time sneaking around watching what I'm doing!'

'Perhaps that's because you're so very watchable,' he suggested, sliding down on to the sand beside her. 'You were what—fifteen?—when we last met, and you've certainly improved by leaps and bounds since then.'

'I've grown up in a lot of other ways, as well,' she retorted. 'And I'm quite capable of looking after myself. I don't need you hanging around like some oversized watchdog!'

Rafe merely shrugged. 'Since you seem determined to stick around, I feel duty-bound to keep an eye on you. Your mother's got a low enough opinion of me as it is. If I let you drown yourself or do something equally stupid, I'd never hear the last of it.'

Kate's muttered reply was fairly incoherent, and Rafe gently raised one eyebrow. 'I didn't quite catch that.'

She hauled herself into a sitting position and shot a black glance in his direction. 'I didn't say anything important.'

He smiled that infuriating smile of his, then he uncoiled himself and got to his feet.

'I think I'll take a swim,' he announced. 'By the way,' he went on in a conversational tone, 'did I mention that I never bother with swimming-trunks?'

'No, you certainly *didn't* mention it,' Kate squeaked.

Rafe shrugged. 'This beach is completely private, so there's no one around to be shocked.'

'*I'm* here,' she reminded him tartly. Then she very hurriedly averted her eyes as he began to unwind the towel from his waist.

'If it bothers you, then you don't have to stick around,' he told her calmly.

Kate willed away the infuriating flush of colour that was threatening to flood her face. 'It doesn't bother me in the least,' she retorted, lying through her teeth. 'I'm not likely to faint with excitement at the sight of a naked male body!'

'Then there's no problem, is there?' he responded in a completely unruffled tone. And with that, he strolled down to the sea, and then began to swim away from the shore with an easy, powerful crawl.

Kate hadn't been able to resist a brief glance, and was left with an uncomfortably vivid image of a powerful male body with broad shoulders, well-shaped, muscular buttocks, and strong thighs.

She swallowed hard a couple of times, and then became increasingly angry at his outrageous behaviour. She was sure that he had done that on purpose. He had known she would be here, and had quite deliberately put on that display of shameless exhibitionism! Her brows drew together in a dark scowl. Was that how he got his kicks? she asked herself with some disgust. As she finally began to cool down again a little, though, she gradually became convinced that it wasn't as simple as that. In fact, she was beginning to suspect that there was a fairly complicated motive behind a lot of the things that Rafe did.

When she had calmed down even further, it wasn't too hard to figure out what his motive had been this time. He had been using his sexuality to try and scare her out of the villa. The big bad wolf playing games with innocent little Red Riding Hood. Well, it wasn't going to work, she muttered to herself with a furious scowl. She might be a bit of an innocent, but she wasn't going to get hysterical and run off because her cousin strutted around naked in front of her!

Then she glanced up and saw that Rafe had begun to swim back towards the shore. Kate quickly scrambled to her feet and scurried away from the beach.

'I'm *not* nervous of him. Of course I'm not,' she insisted under her breath. Then her mouth relaxed into a reluctant grin. 'It's just that there are only so many impressive sights a girl can take in one day!'

She hurried back to the villa, and somehow resisted the urge to turn round for one last quick peep.

CHAPTER THREE

WHEN Kate reached the villa, she headed upstairs to take a shower. As she stood under the hot water she began to wonder why Rafe was trying so hard to hound her out of the villa. She had thought at first that he might have his eye on some gorgeous female, and he didn't want her around because she might cramp his style, but Kate hadn't caught so much as a glimpse of any woman. Unlikely as it seemed, Rafe appeared to be living like a monk at the moment. She was absolutely certain that he was up to *something*, though, and she was getting more and more curious as to what it was.

She dried herself, doused herself with talc, pulled on shorts and a T-shirt, and then headed down to the kitchen for breakfast.

She was a little annoyed to find that Rafe had got there before her. At least he was fully dressed now, though, in denims and a sweatshirt.

'I see you've managed to find some clothes,' she remarked very pointedly.

Rafe put a couple of rashers of bacon into the frying pan, and then stood back slightly as the fat sizzled. 'It's a big mistake to fry food without adequate protection,' he commented, in an unperturbed voice. 'Incidentally, perhaps I ought to warn you—I don't just swim naked, I sleep that way, as well.'

'I don't care if you sleep hanging upside down from the rafters!' she retorted. 'It really makes no difference at all to me.'

Rafe's dark eyes suddenly gleamed. 'It might, if we bumped into each other in the middle of the night,' he suggested silkily.

Kate lifted her nose high into the air. 'If we both stay in our own beds, there's absolutely no possibility of that happening.'

'I don't think it's going to be a lot of fun, having you around,' he remarked regretfully. He cracked a couple of eggs into the pan. 'Want some breakfast?'

'I'm not hungry,' she said haughtily, even though she was starving. 'Anyway, all that greasy food is bad for you. It clogs your arteries and mucks up your digestive system.'

'I think I'll risk it just this once,' Rafe replied cheerfully. 'Sure you don't want some?'

Kate's stomach rumbled hungrily, and she hurriedly coughed to cover it up. 'No, thanks.' She poured herself a glass of fresh juice and picked up an apple. 'I know what's good for me,' she told him.

Rafe's gaze changed quite noticeably as it swivelled round to fix on her. 'Do you?' he queried in a soft tone. 'Then how come you're still sticking around, Kate?'

She decided that she didn't want to answer that question. Instead, she turned her back on him and made a dignified exit.

Nearly an hour later, she heard his car starting up. She shot over to the nearest window, just in time to see the dusty Renault disappearing down the drive. Kate gave a relieved sigh and headed straight for the kitchen, where she raided the fridge and then cooked herself a huge breakfast.

When she had eaten it and cleared away, she decided to take herself off to Nice to do some shopping. Thanks to Great-Uncle Henry she could afford to buy anything she liked, within reason. She didn't intend to fritter the money away, of course, but it would be nice to browse around in some of those exclusive shops and know that she could splash out on some really expensive item, if she wanted to.

She changed into a dress, slid her newly acquired credit cards into her bag, and headed out to her car. Minutes later, she was on the main coast road, and heading towards Nice.

She had gone about a mile when she saw a small, dusty Renault tucked away on the far side of the road. Kate's brows drew together. Was it Rafe's car? It definitely *looked* like it. She couldn't be absolutely certain, though. Anyway, it was none of her business, she reminded herself, and she drove on.

Although it wasn't quite the height of the tourist season, Nice was still full of people—and traffic! Kate didn't mind the bustle, though. It made a welcome change from the tranquillity of the Villa des Anges. At least, it was fairly tranquil whenever Rafe wasn't around! she told herself with a rueful frown.

The shops were full of clothes that were deliciously feminine, but horrifyingly expensive. Kate browsed happily for a couple of hours, but didn't buy anything. She had lunch at an open-air restaurant, and then strolled down the Promenade des Anglais. The sun shone down hotly, the trees which lined the Promenade swayed gently in the breeze, and the flowers blazed with colour. Kate soaked up the sights, sounds and smells, and decided that she was going to love spending the summer here.

It was late afternoon before she wandered back to her car and set off on the drive back to the villa. Curiosity made her look out for the dusty Renault that she had seen that morning, and had thought might be Rafe's. And it was curiosity that made her pull over to the side of the road when she saw that it was still there, in exactly the same position.

'It *is* his,' she muttered to herself as she got close enough to see the number-plate. 'But why is he still here? More to the point, what's he up to?'

The car was parked in the shade of some bushes. A few yards beyond them was a private road, and Kate looked at it thoughtfully. Was that where Rafe had gone? But why?

He might just be visiting a girlfriend, she reasoned with herself. Yet she had the feeling that he was up to more than that. A tiny tingle of excitement ran up her spine. Was this something to do with the reason that Rafe wanted her out of the villa?

'You're never going to find out by just standing around, trying to make guesses,' she told herself. 'Why not take a look?'

She parked her own car behind Rafe's; then, a little nervously, she walked towards the side road. She knew that Rafe definitely wouldn't like it if he discovered that she was spying on him. On the other hand, she was never going to find out what was going on unless she did some snooping around.

The sign at the entrance to the road clearly stated that this was private property. Kate stared at it for a few moments, but then decided to ignore it. Surely no one would mind too much if she just walked down the road for a short distance?

There were thick bushes on either side, and the road twisted quite a lot, so she couldn't see too far ahead. Eventually, though, she rounded one last corner and found herself confronted by tall wrought-iron gates. They were closed, and locked by what looked like a very sophisticated security system, which meant that this was definitely the end of the line.

Rather disappointed, she pressed her face against the gates and could just catch a glimpse of a villa through the trees ahead. It looked far more imposing than the Villa des Anges, and she guessed that it was owned by someone who was seriously rich. This was one of the most exclusive stretches of the coast, where even a small house cost a fortune.

With a small frown, she wondered what business Rafe had at a place like this. She hoped he wasn't messing around with the owner's wife. Anyone who could afford a place like this must have quite a lot of power and influence. Rafe might find himself in serious trouble if he crossed someone like that!

Still wondering what her cousin was up to, she turned away from the gate and began to trudge back down the lane. Preoccupied with her own thoughts, she didn't hear the faint rustle in the bushes behind her, or see the man who slid silently out of the shadows.

A second later, a hand was clamped tightly over her mouth and her arm was twisted efficiently, although not painfully, behind her back.

Kate was instantly paralysed with pure fear. Part of her brain frantically told her that she ought to fight, but her limbs had gone totally limp. She felt herself being dragged backwards into the bushes, and she made a feeble attempt to wriggle free from her attacker, but there was still no strength in her arms or legs. Once they were in the shelter of the bushes, she was flung rather roughly to the ground, and a heavy body dived on top of her. Kate's heart was thumping so fast that she thought it was going to burst, and she kept telling herself that this wasn't happening, it *couldn't* be happening, but the hot, crushing body was real enough, and so were the strong arms that still held her prisoner.

The hand over her mouth eased its grip just a fraction, and she dragged in a gasping breath, determined to yell for help, even though she knew there was no one around to hear her frantic cries.

Her attacker must have realised what she intended doing. *'Quiet!'* rasped Rafe's voice in her ear.

Kate's eyes shot wide open. *Rafe?* It was Rafe doing this to her?

'Not a word,' he grated in a low undertone.

Since Kate was too stunned to get out a single sound, the two of them lay very quietly for a few seconds. Then Kate heard the unmistakable sound of a car passing, very close by.

It stopped a short distance away, and she heard a clanking sound, which she realised was the wrought-iron gates being opened. The car passed through, she heard the gates being closed again, and then it went very quiet.

Rafe released his grip on her. 'Now, perhaps you'd like to tell me just what the hell you're doing here,' he said grimly.

'What *I'm* doing here?' Kate said incredulously, rounding on him. 'I was taking a walk along a quiet road. Of course, I didn't know my half-witted cousin was going to jump out of the bushes and frighten me nearly to death!'

Her voice was shaking, and her body was still trembling. It was going to be a long time—if ever!—before she forgave Rafe for doing this to her.

'Cut the innocent act,' he advised tersely. 'It's a million to one chance that you should just happen to be taking a walk down this particular road.'

'I saw your car,' she told him furiously. 'It looked abandoned, and I—I thought you might be in trouble.' She was a long way from the truth now, but she didn't care. 'I came looking for you, to see if—if you needed help——'

'You were prying, Kate,' he cut in. 'You didn't give a damn if I needed help or not. You just wanted to find out what I was up to.'

'And what if I did?' She glared at him balefully. 'That was still no excuse for jumping on me like that. I thought you were a rapist!'

'If you want to stick your nose into something that's none of your business, then you had better be prepared to take the consequences,' came Rafe's totally unsympathetic reply.

'And what *were* you doing, lurking in those bushes?' she demanded. 'And why did you have to grab hold of me and fling me to the ground? Or do you just like putting on the caveman act?' she accused.

Rafe's expression was dangerously black by now. 'I didn't want those people in the car to see you.'

'Then why didn't you just tell me that?'

'There wasn't time. You'd have wanted explanations, and you'd probably have started to argue with me. It was important that you weren't seen.'

'Why was it important?' she threw back at him.

'This is private property.' An evasive note had crept into his voice. 'You could have been in serious trouble.'

'Rubbish!' she said dismissively. 'I wasn't doing any harm. I simply walked along the lane, peered through the gates, and then began to walk back again. No one's going to prosecute me for that!'

'You don't know these people.'

'And you do?' Curiosity was now beginning to replace the anger in her voice.

Rafe seemed to realise that she was beginning to back him into a corner. 'Whether I do or not, it's nothing to do with you,' he said irritably.

'No? *I* was the one who was flung to the ground,' she reminded him sharply. 'And *I* was the one who was scared half to death. I think I deserve some kind of explanation.'

He scowled at her. 'I've already given you one.'

'No, you haven't,' she flashed back immediately. 'You've not even begun to tell me what you're really doing here.'

'I've told you everything that you need to know.' He caught hold of her elbow and steered her towards the road. 'Let's get back to the villa. There's not much point in hanging around here any longer.'

Kate allowed him to hustle her along, but at the same time she stared at him suspiciously. 'You know what I think?' she challenged. 'You're not here on holiday at all. You're on a job—something to do with your enquiry agency. And I reckon it's all tied up with the people who live in that villa behind the locked gates.'

'Don't ask any more questions, Kate,' he advised grimly. 'And don't try to get mixed up in it. In fact, why don't you just pack your things and head back home to England, where you belong?'

But nothing on earth would have persuaded Kate to do that, not now. She didn't ask any more questions out loud, but that didn't mean there weren't dozens of them buzzing around inside her head. And, one way or another, she was totally determined to get to the bottom of this.

Kate didn't sleep well that night, and woke up the next morning to another scorchingly hot day. She had a slight headache, and she padded over to the window, opened it, and leant out. The fresh air made her feel better almost immediately, and she gave a faint sigh of satisfaction. Despite all the hassle with Rafe, she loved it here, and she was really looking forward to the rest of the summer.

Then she let out a snort of annoyance as she saw Rafe coming up the path that led from the beach. Trust him to turn up and ruin a perfectly good morning!

He glanced up and saw her, and then aimed an unexpectedly lazy smile in her direction. Kate didn't return it, though. Instead, she was a little horrified to find herself wondering what—if anything!—he was wearing beneath the towel that was casually hooked around his waist.

This man is provoking you into perverted thoughts! she lectured herself sternly. He's definitely a bad influence, Kate. You ought to stay away from him.

The only trouble was, that wasn't particularly easy when they were both living under the same roof. If anyone was going to move out, then it was pretty obvious that it would have to be her. Kate had already decided that she was staying, though. Rafe was up to something—perhaps even something not very legal—and she intended to find out what it was.

He was still grinning at her, as if the events of yesterday hadn't even happened. 'If you'd woken up a little earlier, you could have joined me for a swim,' he called up.

'Thanks, but that's one experience I'm happy to do without,' she retorted. 'There are certain sights that are guaranteed to put you right off your breakfast!'

Rafe casually slid the towel from around his waist. 'I'm wearing swimming-trunks this morning,' he informed her with gentle mockery. 'I didn't want to offend your delicate sensibilities. In fact, if you stay much longer, I might even end up wearing pyjamas to bed at night.'

'Don't bother on my account,' she batted back at him. 'You can walk around clothed from head to toe, or stark naked. Either way, it doesn't worry me in the least.'

'Then why did you go that rather odd colour just now, when I removed the towel?' enquired Rafe with interest.

'I did not!' Kate retorted hotly. 'And stop *laughing* at me.'

She slammed the window shut so that she wouldn't have to see his grinning face or put up with any more of those sly comments that so got under her skin.

'I hope a few sharks turn up next time he goes swimming!' she muttered under her breath. Then she headed off to the shower in a thoroughly bad temper.

When she finally made her way downstairs, there was no sign of Rafe. She fed the cats, had her own breakfast, and was just about to wander out on to the terrace with a cup of coffee when the phone rang.

For a moment, she considered ignoring it. Then she gave a small sigh, put down her coffee, walked over to the phone and picked up the receiver.

A smile spread over her face as she heard her father's voice at the other end, and she was glad she had answered it. His familiar tones made her realise that she was, in fact, just a little bit homesick.

'I don't have to be at the office until later this morning, so I thought I'd give you a quick ring. How's it going, Kate?'

'Fine,' she replied, rather too brightly. 'The weather's still gorgeous, the villa's marvellous, and I'm having a really good time.'

'Is Rafe still there?'

'Yes, he is,' she said, her voice more guarded now.

'And is he having a good time, as well?'

'I suppose so—at least, as far as I know. We don't have a great deal of contact.' That wasn't the exact truth, but she didn't want her father to worry about her. Anyway, it all depended on how you defined the word 'contact'. Being slung over Rafe's shoulder, or hauled into the bushes and then having him dive on top of you was certainly contact of a sort! She didn't think it would be a good idea to tell her father about those particular episodes, though.

'Are you going to stay at the villa for the rest of the summer?' asked her father. 'We miss having you around.'

'And I miss you,' Kate admitted. 'But I think it's high time I learnt to stand on my own two feet.'

'Well, don't forget that we're here if you need us. By the way, here's your mother. I think she wants a word with you.' His voice lowered a fraction. 'Kate, I'm afraid I mentioned that——'

He obviously didn't get a chance to finish what he had been about to say, because the next voice Kate heard was her mother's.

'Kate? Is it true that Rafe's staying at the villa with you?' she demanded.

Kate let out a silent sigh. She should have remembered that her father found it very hard to keep secrets from her mother.

'Well—in a way—yes,' she confirmed cautiously.

'You're to come home at once!' her mother instructed. 'I don't want any daughter of mine staying under the same roof as that man.'

'There's absolutely nothing to worry about,' Kate said very firmly.

Her mother gave a disbelieving snort. 'Of course there is! You need to be twice your age and three times as experienced to cope with someone like Rafe.'

'How can you say that, when you don't really know him?' Kate asked a little impatiently.

'I know *about* him.'

'That's just gossip. I don't suppose half of it's true.'

'Well, if even a fraction of it is true, that's enough for me!' came her mother's instant reply. 'You're to get a flight back home as soon as you can.'

But Kate had spent much of her life automatically obeying her mother, and she had decided that it had to stop. She loved her mother, but recognised that there was a domineering side to her character. Kate had accepted it, and all too often given in to it—as her father did—for the sake of a quiet life. She was twenty-two years old now, though, and it was definitely time she took charge of her own life.

'I'm staying right here,' she announced firmly. 'Rafe isn't a problem, and even if he were I'd be able to handle him.' Which might not be strictly the truth, but Kate wasn't going to admit that to anyone except herself.

'I'm sorry, Kate, but it's just not on,' argued her mother. 'I insist that you come back home.'

'Mum, I'm not a kid any more,' Kate reminded her, although not unkindly. 'You can't insist that I do anything.'

There was a short silence from the other end of the phone, as if that statement hadn't gone down at all well.

'Headstrong,' came her mother's resigned comment, at last. 'It's the Clarendon blood coming out in you. You get it from your father, of course. What a pity you didn't take after my side of the family.'

Kate heard the front door of the villa opening, and she lowered her voice a fraction. 'Look, I've got to go. Someone's just come in——'

'Is it Rafe?' demanded her mother. 'I want to speak to him, Kate. There are quite a few things I want to say to that man——'

'He's—he's already gone upstairs,' Kate lied hastily. 'Must go, Mum. Love to all, and I'll ring you in a couple of days.'

She hastily put down the receiver before her mother could get out another word. Rafe strolled over, and looked at her enquiringly.

'It was my mother on the phone,' Kate explained. 'She—she sends you her regards.'

Rafe's eyebrows shot up in clear disbelief. 'Her *regards*?' he echoed.

'Well—that might not have been the *exact* word she used,' admitted Kate.

'I'm sure it wasn't,' he said drily. 'Your mother seems to think I'm some sort of cross between Casanova and Bluebeard.'

'A virgin for breakfast every morning?' suggested Kate, with a grin.

'Something like that.'

'But that's a bit of an exaggeration?'

'Life's rarely that exciting.' He glanced at his watch. 'I'm going out now, and I probably won't be back for the rest of the day. Will you be all right here, on your own?'

'Of course I'll be all right,' she said, a little impatiently. 'I told you before, I'm not a child. I don't need you around to hold my hand.'

His gaze slid appreciatively over her. 'No, you're certainly not a child,' he agreed, and something in his tone made the fine hairs on Kate's skin stand right up on end.

She raised her head and glared at him, annoyed that he could provoke this sort of reaction from her. 'And where exactly are you going?' she demanded. 'No, don't tell me. Let me guess. You're going to spend the day spying on those people at the villa.'

Rafe's eyes grew very cool. 'I warned you yesterday not to ask any more questions. Don't cross me about this, Kate, or you might not like the consequences.'

He turned round and strode out before she had a chance to say another word. Kate scowled at his retreating back. His moods changed faster than the English weather!

True to his word, he didn't come back to the Villa des Anges until late in the day. He stayed just long enough to have a quick meal, and then went straight out again. This time, Kate didn't even bother to ask him where he was going. If she wanted to find out what he was up to, she knew that she was going to have to be a lot more subtle about it.

When she finally took herself off to bed, Rafe still hadn't returned. Because she had had a restless night the night before, she was tired and fell asleep fairly quickly. A couple of hours later, though, she surfaced back into wakefulness. As she lay there in the darkness, she licked her lips. Her mouth felt dry, and she was longing for a drink.

Since she didn't feel in the least sleepy any more, she hauled herself out of bed and padded downstairs, the floor deliciously cool against her bare feet. She made her way to the kitchen, drank some fruit juice, and then glanced at her watch. It was two in the morning. Kate wrinkled her nose. She still felt wide awake, but she supposed she had better go back to bed and try to get some sleep. She flicked off the light, made her way through the dark hall, and had just reached the foot of the stairs when the lock on the front door suddenly clicked. Then the door itself swung open. Kate immediately gulped. A burglar? she asked herself shakily. Then she relaxed again. A burglar would hardly be letting himself in with a key!

There was a small lamp on the table at the foot of the stairs. Kate reached over and switched it on; then she looked up again to find that Rafe had just walked in through the door.

He was wearing dark jeans and a black sweatshirt, and looked extremely tired. Kate didn't feel in the least sorry for him, though. Whatever he had been up to, she was sure it was something underhand. It served him right if he was nearly asleep on his feet.

When Rafe saw her standing there, one dark eyebrow lifted speculatively.

'You're up late,' he commented.

'And you're *in* late,' she shot back meaningfully.

'Yes, I am,' he agreed, stifling a yawn. 'And I didn't expect to find you waiting up for me.' His eyes suddenly glinted. '*Are* you waiting up for me, Kate?' he queried with some interest.

'No, I am not!' she denied vehemently.

'That's a shame. I'm definitely in the mood for some female company right now. And I happen to like women who are dark-haired, dark-eyed and bad-tempered.' His sleepy voice had taken on an unexpectedly silky note, and Kate was instantly on her guard.

'I'm not bad-tempered!' she snapped back at him. 'At least, not usually,' she said, a little more defensively. 'It's just that you get right under my skin a lot of the time!'

'That sounds like a very pleasant place to be,' he murmured. Then he gave an enormous yawn. 'Hell, I'm tired. That's probably why I'm waffling on like this. I often talk nonsense when I'm tired.'

Kate relaxed just a fraction. 'So do I. And don't worry, I'm not taking much notice. I know you're not being serious. I mean, you wouldn't want to—want...'

Her voice trailed away rather uncertainly as Rafe's eyes suddenly looked very much less sleepy than they had a moment ago.

'Wouldn't want to what?' he questioned her softly. 'Kiss you, perhaps? But I rather think that I would, Kate.'

'Just cut that out,' she said edgily. Then her curiosity got the better of her. 'Why on earth do you like women who are bad-tempered?' she couldn't help asking.

Rafe grinned. 'It just makes things more interesting. I've never liked a quiet life. And I certainly wouldn't want to live with someone who was passive and amenable all the time. I'd be bored to death in a week.' Then his dark eyes suddenly flared again. 'I'm beginning to think that you wouldn't bore me, Kate,' he added softly.

Kate took an involuntary step backwards. 'You're starting to talk nonsense again,' she warned him.

'Am I? But don't you think it might be nice to try it for a couple of minutes?' he said persuasively. 'You might even find that you enjoy it.'

The sheer arrogance of the man infuriated her. What did he think she was going to do? Swoon with delight as soon as he got her into his arms?

'I don't intend to give you a couple of seconds, let alone a couple of minutes,' she informed him tartly. 'And if you'd just get out of my way, I'd like to go up to——' she nearly said 'bed', but at the last moment hurriedly altered it '——to my room,' she finished, glaring at him.

To her surprise, he immediately stepped aside, leaving her a clear passage up the stairs. Kate's muscles sagged with relief. Until that moment, she hadn't realised just how tense she had become, waiting to see what move Rafe was going to make next.

Somehow, she restrained the urge to scuttle past him. She definitely didn't want him to think she was frightened of him! Instead, she went up the first couple of stairs at a steady pace, with her nose held high in the air. She would simply ignore him. That was the best way—probably the *only* way—to deal with someone like Rafe.

She thought she had got away with it. She had gone past him now, and the empty stairway stretched ahead of her. If only she could bound up it, she thought regretfully, then she put that tempting thought to one side. Retreat with a little dignity! she told herself. At the same time, she released a silent sigh of relief. This wasn't turning out as bad as she had thought it would be.

An instant later, though, Rafe's arm snaked out and curled round her waist. Then he pulled her backwards, so that she tumbled towards him. He deftly caught her, and restored her balance. Then he easily fielded her fist, which she had instinctively aimed straight towards his jaw. His fingers closed round it, holding her entire arm immobile, and he shot a reproving look at her.

'That's not a wise thing to do, Kate. Some men are turned on by that sort of aggressiveness. Luckily for you, I'm not one of them.'

'Oh, sure, I'm a really lucky girl,' she agreed sarcastically. 'Stuck here with you, in the middle of the night! Well, if you're not turned on, I'd appreciate it if you'd let go of me!'

'Oh, I didn't say I wasn't turned on,' he responded in a soft tone that sent shivers from the top to the very bottom of her spine. 'And I think I'd rather like that kiss I wanted earlier.'

His mouth smoothly closed over hers before she could get out the very vociferous protest that she had intended. Kate gurgled incoherently, and was then forced to concentrate solely on trying to breathe. Her brows began to draw together a little frantically. Didn't the wretched man realise that he was suffocating her?

Apparently he did, because his kiss eased off a little. Oxygen rushed into Kate's lungs, and she slumped with relief. Another few seconds of that, and she might have blacked out!

Rafe still hadn't let go of her, though. In fact, if anything his grip had tightened a fraction. And his fingers were playing subtle rhythms against the line of her spine. She didn't like that. At least, she didn't think she did. It made her nerve-ends tingle in a way that was half pleasant and half disturbing.

'Stop it,' she mumbled.

'Stop what?' enquired Rafe, a little breathlessly.

'Everything!' she retorted.

'Wasn't there one single thing that you enjoyed? That you'd like to do again?' he said persuasively.

'No!' she lied.

'Then perhaps I'd better try something else.' His dark gaze seemed to have become quite black. 'I never like to admit defeat.'

His fingers slid under her hair, finally finding the warm, vulnerable skin at the nape of her neck. They traced delicate patterns there for a while, and Kate was horrified to find that she was actually beginning to relax. With a huge effort, she forced her muscles to tense up again.

'Why do that?' murmured Rafe. 'You're only spoiling it.'

'How can you spoil something that was never all that great in the first place?' she demanded.

'That's because you won't *let* it be great. Like it or not, Kate, we could be very good together.'

Kate's skin began to grow cold with the first pricklings of apprehension. Except for her and Rafe, the villa was empty. Any kind of help was a million miles away. She kept trying to convince herself that Rafe wouldn't hurt her, wouldn't force her into anything. He was her cousin, for heaven's sake! She was quite safe with him.

But he isn't really your cousin, a shaky voice inside her head reminded her. And just think of all the stories you've heard about him—and none of them were good!

Without any warning, Rafe swung her round, so that she had her back to the wall. Then he kept her pinned in place by the simple expedient of placing his body directly in front of her. Since he was bigger and stronger, there was no way of escape until he chose to let her go.

'Scared?' he challenged softly, studying her face very closely. 'Perhaps you ought to be, Kate. You've caught me at a bad moment. I'm tired, and I'm in an odd mood. And now I've started something that I'm finding it very hard to stop.'

Even before he had finished speaking, his hands had begun to move again, and in deadly earnest this time. Her thin cotton nightie was no protection against him. She could feel the warmth of his palms and the probing of his fingertips as clearly as if she had been stark naked.

Kate gulped hard and closed her eyes a trifle desperately. Perhaps if she pretended this just wasn't happening...

Rafe's mouth moved against the side of her throat, and her eyes shot wide open. That definitely wasn't going to work! And, oh, heavens, something inside her just seemed to be *melting*, and she was horrified to find that she liked it, wanted more of it...

It seemed that Rafe was only too happy to oblige. He made no effort to remove her nightdress, but seemed content to let that flimsy barrier remain in place, as if he got a perverse pleasure out of being frustrated in his desire to explore further.

He turned his attention back to her lips, and this time he left her with plenty of opportunity to breathe. Only it was still difficult, because Kate's lungs were wheezing by this time, constricted by something she didn't even begin to understand.

His tongue delicately probed. Then he withdrew for a few seconds. 'Do you like this, Kate?' he enquired in a slightly rough voice.

'No,' she denied, a little frantically, but Rafe merely smiled.

'I'm sure your parents would be completely shocked if they knew you were capable of telling such a massive lie.' His fingers moved again, turning their attention to the hot, swollen line of her breast. 'Are you beginning to ache yet?' he murmured in a very different tone.

Kate shakily decided that there wasn't much point in denying it any longer. She had a healthy young body, and it was sending out clear signals that it was *very* interested in Rafe Clarendon. Even someone with half his experience would be able to read those signals quite easily.

'Of course I'm reacting,' she muttered, relieved to find that her voice sounded a lot more steady than her trembling limbs. 'You're very good at this, aren't you? But then, I dare say you've had a lot of practice. There must have been dozens of women in your life!'

'Dozens,' agreed Rafe, without batting an eyelid. 'At least, according to your mother, and all the assorted aunts and great-aunts who love to gossip about me.'

Kate looked at him guardedly. 'Then it isn't true?'

His eyes flashed with sudden amusement. 'I didn't say that.'

'Oh, you're so annoying!' she said, with a faint scowl.

'I'm also a little insane for letting this situation get so out of control,' he said ruefully. 'This is hardly the way to get rid of you!'

'Oh, I don't know,' Kate retorted, with a touch of her old spirit. 'I might have hated it so much that I'll be packing my bags and leaving first thing in the morning.'

His gaze rested on her reflectively. 'But you won't, will you, Kate?'

'No, I won't,' she said, with great firmness. 'If all this was just a ruse to get me out of here, then it hasn't worked.'

'Oh, it wasn't a ruse,' he told her evenly. 'And that's the trouble. You're starting to complicate my life in more ways than one.'

'We could just forget about tonight,' she suggested, although she knew very well that it was going to be a long time before she could erase it from her own memory. 'It needn't be a problem.'

Rafe began to look restless. 'Just having you here is a problem. And I don't mean because of what's happened between us tonight, although that's certainly not helped the situation. It would be much better all round if you just moved out of the villa, Kate.'

'You mean better for you! Well, I'm not going until you give me a very good reason *why* I should go,' she said stubbornly. Rafe shifted away from her, which gave her a chance to pull herself together and think more clearly. 'I know you don't want me out of here just because of tonight,' she went on. 'And I know you're not really here on holiday. I *don't* know why you're being so uptight and secretive about the whole thing, though, or why you don't want me around.'

'Believe me, it would be far better if you knew nothing about it.' He prowled even further away from her. 'You're right, I'm not here on holiday,' he finally admitted with some reluctance. 'I've come to France on behalf of a client. But I'm not working on an ordinary case right now. It isn't even very legal. That's why I want you well away from here, in case the whole thing blows up in my face.'

But Kate was far too intrigued now to let it go at that. 'I'm not even going to think about leaving this villa until you tell me exactly what's going on. And even then, I might decide to stick around.'

'You're a Clarendon, all right,' he said, with a touch of exasperation. 'Stubborn through and through!' Then his expression changed. 'But if it's the only chance I've got to get rid of you, then I suppose I'm going to have to tell you what I'm up to. But you're not going to like it, Kate.'

'Try me,' she invited.

He gave a faint groan. 'Don't tempt me! My resistance is pretty low right now.' He stood with his back to her for a while, and when he at last swung back to face her his expression was very different from what it had been only seconds ago. 'On the other hand, when you know why I'm here you might not want me to come near you ever again.' Rafe looked at her very steadily. 'You see, I've come to France for just one reason. I'm going to try and kidnap a six-year-old boy.'

CHAPTER FOUR

KATE was sure she had misheard him. He couldn't possibly have said that he intended to kidnap someone!

Rafe studied her face rather tensely. 'You don't believe me? Then perhaps we'd better leave it at that.'

'No,' she said sharply, with an abrupt shake of her head. 'No—if you really mean it, then I want to hear about it. You can't just walk off without telling me more.'

'Then go and put some clothes on first,' he instructed. 'That thin nightdress is just too damned distracting. I can't think straight while you're wearing it.'

With her head dazed from both his kisses and his startling announcement, Kate trailed slowly up the stairs. Perhaps he had been joking, she told herself confusedly. Yet she knew from the look on his face that he hadn't been.

She pulled on jeans and a T-shirt, and then reluctantly went back downstairs. She wasn't at all sure that she wanted to hear whatever Rafe was going to tell her. All her instincts were warning her that this could well lead to big trouble.

Rafe was waiting for her in the kitchen. 'Want some coffee?' he offered, as she came through the door.

'Coffee?' she repeated, a little incredulously. 'You tell me that you're planning to kidnap a small boy, and then you calmly offer me coffee?'

He shrugged. 'Personally, I need it. I'm nearly asleep on my feet, and I've a feeling that you're not going to let me go to bed until we've gone into this in some detail.'

'You're right about that,' she retorted. 'I mean, I know you've got a reputation for doing slightly crazy things, but I never thought you'd go in for anything like this!'

'Neither did I,' he said drily. He poured himself some coffee, and then sat down at the table. 'Take a seat,' he invited, gesturing to the chair opposite. 'This could take some time.'

'Thanks, but I prefer to stand,' Kate told him stiffly. She moved to the far side of the kitchen. Then she realised that she hadn't wanted to take that seat because she didn't want to get too near to him. Quite suddenly, Rafe didn't seem like the same man who had kissed and caressed her such a short time ago.

'I suppose you want to know how I got involved in all this,' he said.

'Not really,' Kate said in a disapproving tone. 'I guess that, in your line of work, you'll tackle anything as long as it pays well.'

Some of the tiredness left Rafe's face, and his eyes glinted dangerously. 'Believe it or not, I do have certain standards. There are plenty of jobs I've turned down because they were too dirty or downright illegal.'

'But obviously you don't mind tackling a little kidnapping,' she retaliated. 'Especially when it's a small boy who'll be fairly easy to snatch, and won't put up too much of a fight!'

'Don't judge me until you know all the facts!' Rafe said sharply. Then he made an obvious effort to calm himself. 'Don't you think I've gone over all the pros and cons a hundred times? Normally, I never touch anything that's outside the law, and I've never even considered doing anything like this before.'

'Then why do it now? Short of money?' she said with some contempt.

His face became positively thunderous. 'I thought you wanted to know the facts! You haven't even heard them, and yet you're already judging me and making me out to be some kind of villain.'

'Well, I don't see that you can blame me!' Kate retorted. 'What possible kind of justification can you come up with for kidnapping a young child?'

'How about the fact that he's already been snatched away from his mother, and she's absolutely desperate to get him back again?' he challenged tautly.

Kate looked at him warily. 'Snatched by whom?'

'His father,' Rafe replied bluntly.

She gave a disbelieving groan. 'Rafe, you haven't got mixed up in one of these tug-of-love cases? You can't be that crazy! These things have to be settled legally. You can't just grab a child from one parent and hand it over to another.'

Rafe slammed his fist down on the table, making her jump violently. 'Don't keep making judgements. This case *was* settled legally. The judge awarded the mother full custody, after she and the boy's father were divorced. The boy himself wanted to stay with his mother, and the judge went along with that. The father was granted visiting rights, but that was all.'

'So, what went wrong?'

'The father wouldn't accept the judge's ruling. He fought it right through the courts and, when he still lost, he took matters into his own hands and just snatched the boy from his mother.'

Kate frowned. 'How did he get away with it?'

'Because he's got money and power and influence,' Rafe stated baldly. 'When you're armed with those three things, you can get away with all sorts of things, even though they're quite illegal.'

Her brows drew even deeper together. 'The boy—is he staying at that villa you were watching the other day?'

'Yes. I caught a glimpse of him a couple of mornings ago—he's definitely there. That villa belongs to the boy's father, Martin Foster. It's just one of half a dozen luxury homes he's got scattered throughout the world.'

'Well, if you know where he is, why don't you just tell the mother? Then she can pursue the matter through the French courts. That's got to be better than putting the poor kid through the trauma of another snatch,' she argued hotly.

'Legal proceedings take a long time. Before it ever got to court, Martin Foster would have moved on, taking the boy with him. And next time, we might not be able to find him so easily—if at all.'

'Surely the police could make sure he stays in the country until the case gets to court?'

Rafe gave a cynical smile. 'Martin Foster's a very powerful man. He'd somehow find a way of getting himself and the boy out of the country.'

Kate shook her head decisively. 'But snatching him back can't be the answer. It isn't right, Rafe.'

'None of this has been right, from the very beginning,' he replied rather grimly. 'I'm just trying to straighten it out as best I can, while hurting everyone as little as possible—especially the boy. And I haven't even made any definite decisions yet about trying to grab the boy. I'm going to try and find a way of seeing him. If he seems reasonably happy where he is, then I won't do anything at all. There's no point in uprooting him from a secure home for a second time.'

'The mother won't like that,' warned Kate.

'No, she won't, but it's one of the conditions on which I took the job in the first place.'

'Why isn't the mother here? If you do grab the boy, it would be much better if she was around, so he could be handed straight over to her. That way, he wouldn't be nearly as frightened or confused.'

'That's true,' agreed Rafe. 'But there's always the risk that the father, Martin Foster, might somehow catch a glimpse of her. If that happened, he'd simply move on and we'd have no way of knowing where he'd gone. At the moment, he thinks the mother's pursuing the case through legal means. Since that's usually a fairly long process, he must feel reasonably safe for the time being. That gives us an advantage that I don't want to lose.'

Kate decided that she did, after all, want to sit down. Her legs were suddenly beginning to feel uncomfortably weak.

'I still think you're crazy,' she said. 'You're acting outside the law, and you're going up against a man who's probably got enough power to break you.'

'I'm not afraid of Martin Foster,' Rafe replied calmly. 'And he's the one who acted outside the law in the first place, by snatching the boy. But there could certainly be trouble, and that's why I want you out of it, Kate.'

'You've already tried to throw me out a couple of times,' she reminded him. 'And it didn't work.'

'You didn't know all the facts then. You didn't know *why* I wanted you out of the villa. I suppose I should have been straight with you from the very beginning, but I thought the less you knew about this, the better. Now you can see why you've got to go, though.'

Kate's eyebrows shot up. 'I certainly can't! In fact, I think you're going to need me to stick around.'

'For what?' Rafe questioned sharply.

'If you do grab the boy, then the poor kid's going to be scared to death. He's going to need a woman around. No offence, Rafe, but I shouldn't think you know the first thing about young children.'

'And you do? You're an only child, Kate. You probably know as little about a six-year-old boy as I do.'

'But I'm a female,' she retorted. 'We're meant to have maternal instincts and all that. Anyway, I can't just go back home and forget about all this. I wouldn't be able to sleep at nights, wondering what was happening to that poor kid.'

Rafe looked at her thoughtfully. 'You've suddenly changed your attitude, haven't you? A couple of minutes ago, you were telling me I was crazy to get mixed up in this. Now, you seem to be telling me that you actually want to help.'

She gave a small shrug. 'I don't know the rights and wrongs of this case. I don't even know if there are any. But whatever happens someone's got to be around to look after that kid, and make sure he comes out of this with as few scars as possible.'

'And you're volunteering for that role?'

Kate was quite sure that this was the maddest thing she had ever done in her entire life, but she didn't see how she could back down now. 'It looks like it,' she said, after a brief pause.

'No, Kate,' he said, quietly but firmly. 'I know you mean well, but you don't understand what's involved—or how nasty it could get.'

'I understand that there's a six-year-old boy caught up in the middle of this,' she said indignantly. 'He's probably homesick, scared to death, and wondering what on earth's going to happen next. I'm not going to walk away from this until I know he's all right.'

Rafe's gaze fixed on her. 'And what if we find that the boy isn't at all homesick, or missing his mother? That he's perfectly happy where he is, and having a whale of a time with his father?'

'You've already answered that question. You said you'd let him stay where he was.'

'And you'd go along with that decision? You wouldn't rush in and single-handedly try to restore him to his mother?'

'Of course not,' she said a little indignantly. 'I'm not stupid!'

Rafe got to his feet. 'Then at least we're in agreement on a couple of things. Perhaps we'd better just leave it at that, for now.'

'But what about plans?' she demanded. 'I want to know what you're going to do next.'

'The only plans I've got right now are for a good night's sleep,' he told her.

Kate realised that his tone had suddenly become rather evasive.

'You're not going to let me get involved in this, are you?' she said bluntly.

Rafe paused for only a moment. 'No, I'm not. I shouldn't even have told you about it. This isn't the kind of thing you should get caught up in, Kate.'

'Give me one reason why not!' she demanded.

A faint smile touched the corners of his mouth. 'For one thing, your mother would probably have me hung, drawn and quartered if I allowed anything to happen to her precious daughter. For another——' He looked at her with an expression that she couldn't quite fathom. 'For another, *I* don't want you involved,' he finished.

'Because you think I'll be a hindrance?' she said heatedly.

His face became even more unreadable. 'No, that isn't the reason at all.'

'Then what is?'

But he obviously wasn't going to be drawn on the subject any more tonight. He walked over to the doorway, and stopped there for just a moment, his dark gaze resting on her briefly. 'I've said—and done—a lot of things tonight that I shouldn't have. I'm already regretting it, and in the morning I'll probably be regretting it even more.' Then his tense mouth relaxed a fraction. 'And now, you'd better let me go up to bed alone, or we could end up with even more problems. Goodnight, Kate.'

She started to say something, but then hurriedly stopped herself as she caught the bright glint of his eyes. And she waited until the sound of his footsteps had completely died away before switching off the light and making her own way up the stairs.

Back in her own bed again, Kate found it quite impossible to sleep. All she could seem to think about was what it would be like to be six years old, and be suddenly snatched away from your mother, your home, and everything that was familiar.

She gave a small shiver. She supposed it was every child's nightmare to suddenly lose the love and security that had always surrounded them.

Was Rafe right to try and snatch the child back again? She just didn't know. The whole situation was highly disturbing, and she didn't see how it could be easily resolved without a lot of people getting hurt.

As her thoughts drifted back to Rafe, she found herself remembering the kisses he had given her earlier, and the firm, sure touch of his hands. Then she shivered all over again, but for a very different reason. It was just one more complication, and one that she could well do without right now. Perhaps it would be best to do as he had said, and go back home before this whole thing became even more disturbing.

But you can't do that, she reminded herself. Not until you know what's going to happen to that kid. Just forget your own mixed-up feelings for a while. The only important thing is to try and make sure that the boy comes out of this all right.

She finally managed to grab a couple of hours of sleep just before dawn. She woke up again with a small start, and for a few moments wondered why she felt so confused and unsettled. Then it hit her like a small bomb exploding inside her head. Rafe was going to kidnap a six-year-old boy! And in a moment of insanity she had offered to help him.

Kate groaned out loud. She didn't believe any of this was really happening!

And how about those kisses Rafe gave you last night? murmured a small voice inside her head. Were they a figment of your imagination, as well?

Kate gave another groan as she crawled out of bed. Then she headed for the shower, turned it to cold, and forced herself to step under it. As the icy water hit her warm skin she gave a small yelp, but didn't move. More than at any other time in her life, she needed to be completely awake and with all her wits about her.

A few minutes later, she was covered with goose-pimples, but very definitely wide awake. She had also had time to think things over and reach a couple of clear decisions. She hurriedly dried herself and got dressed, then she headed downstairs.

Rafe was sitting out on the terrace, drinking black coffee. Kate sat herself down in front of him, and looked him straight in the eyes.

'You can't go ahead with this, Rafe,' she told him bluntly.

His face wore a dark expression, and he didn't look particularly pleased to see her.

'I'm the one who'll make the final decision about it,' he growled back at her. 'And, whatever I decide, I don't want you interfering.'

Her own gaze flashed hotly. 'You've rather changed your attitude since last night, haven't you?'

Rafe looked even more ill-tempered. 'Last night was a mistake. All it's done is complicate matters. I shouldn't have told you about my plans—and I certainly shouldn't have touched you. I wouldn't have done if I hadn't been so damned tired. I was just operating on automatic pilot. I saw something I wanted, and I tried to grab it.' His mouth set into a grim line. 'It was a bad mistake, Kate—for both of us.'

'I'm not worried about that right now,' she replied, although she was well aware that she wasn't being very truthful. 'All I care about is what happens to that boy. You can't mess up his life still further. It's nothing to do with you. You've got no right——'

He suddenly sat up much straighter and caught hold of her wrist. 'Then what am I meant to do?' he demanded tersely. 'Leave that kid in a place where he's probably completely miserable and unhappy? Just walk away and forget about it?'

'That might be best,' she argued stubbornly.

'Best for who? Best for me, because it'll mean I'll be spared a lot of hassle and trouble? Best for his mother, who's so desperate to get her child back that she's willing to try just about anything? Yes, you're right, Kate,' he went on in a hard voice. 'It would be a lot more convenient just to drop the whole thing, but I'm not going to do it. Not yet. I want to see that boy first, and find out for myself what sort of state he's in. That's the only way I can decide what to do next—if anything.'

Kate gave a small sigh, and a lot of the fight drained out of her. She had known all along that it would be impossible to persuade Rafe to change his mind. She had had to have a go, though. And now she had failed it was time to move on to the next decision she had made.

'If you're determined to go ahead, then I'm going to stick around and help,' she said firmly.

'No.' Rafe's reply was quiet, but extremely decisive.

'I'm not saying that I want to take part in anything illegal. And if there's a chance of any physical violence, then you can definitely count me out. But it could be useful to have me around at times,' she argued. 'If you want to see the boy, you're going to have to get into Martin Foster's villa, and he's going to be a lot less suspicious of a couple than of a single man hovering around. Think about it, Rafe. It makes a lot of sense.'

She saw him hesitate. It was only for a moment, though.

'I can do this on my own, Kate.'

'I'm sure you can. I'm just saying that there are times when I could help you.'

Rafe shook his head. 'You don't know what you're volunteering for.'

'Of course I do,' she said rather impatiently. 'I'm not an idiot!'

'No, you're not,' he agreed with a sudden dry smile. 'But I still can't go along with it. Thanks for the offer, Kate, and I know you mean well——'

'Mean well?' she repeated in a furious tone. 'Let's get this straight. I'm not some do-gooder. I just want to make sure that you make the right decision about that kid. If he's really unhappy, then I suppose you've got no choice except to try and get him out of there. But if he's OK, and you still want to grab him, then I'll fight you tooth and nail over it.' She glared at him heatedly. 'Do you understand what I'm saying?'

'I certainly do,' he replied wryly. 'By heavens, you *are* a Clarendon. Pushy and obstinate.' Somehow, though, he didn't make it sound like an insult.

'So, what do you say?' she challenged him directly. 'Are you going to let me stick around for a while?'

An unexpected look of resignation came over his face. 'It doesn't look as if I have a choice. But at the first sign of real trouble you're to clear out of here straight away,' he warned.

Kate was more than willing to go along with those terms. She didn't want to get involved in anything that was physically dangerous.

'Where do we begin?' she asked.

'By making an attempt to see the boy, I suppose. But that's easier said than done.'

'Can't we find some excuse for turning up at the villa?'

Rafe shrugged. 'Sure. We could try one of the old favourites, such as saying our car's broken down, and asking to use the phone. There's no guarantee that we'll get to see the boy, though. All Martin Foster has to do is to keep him well out of the way until we've left again.'

Kate's brows drew together. 'Can't we get in *without* an invitation?' she suggested at last.

'A little illegal breaking and entering?' queried Rafe, with raised eyebrows. 'Certainly not! I don't want to spend the next few months in a French gaol. Anyway, you saw the security system on the gates. They've almost certainly got an equally sophisticated system covering the grounds and the villa itself. We wouldn't get any distance before we were picked up.'

Kate was rather annoyed that he had dismissed her suggestions so quickly. 'All right, *you* suggest something.'

Rafe tapped his fingers together slowly. 'The villa has its own private beach,' he said at last. 'According to his mother, the boy loves swimming. There's a good chance he goes down there at some time during the day.'

'Can we reach the beach?' she asked with fresh eagerness.

'There's no direct access. We'd have to go further up the coast, and then swim along to it.'

'I'm willing to try it,' she said at once. 'I'm a good swimmer.'

'I know that.' He looked at her quizzically. 'You're very eager to get yourself into what could be a whole lot of trouble.'

'The sooner we get this settled, the better it'll be for the boy. When can we try it?'

Rafe glanced at his watch. 'It's rather late to make a start on anything today. If the boy does go swimming, it's more likely to be in the morning. By the time we get there, it'll be nearly midday. We'd better leave it until tomorrow.' He lifted his gaze and looked at her. 'That swimsuit you wore the other morning—is it the only one you've got?'

'No,' she said, a trifle puzzled. 'I've another one that's very similar, but a different colour.'

'Mmm.' He reached into his pocket, pulled out his wallet, and handed her a small wad of notes. 'Go into Nice this afternoon, and buy yourself a bikini. Something very brief and sexy.'

Kate stared at him indignantly. 'What for?'

'Because if that boy does come to the beach, I'm pretty certain he won't be on his own. My guess is that he'll have some sort of bodyguard. It might be helpful if you could somehow—distract the bodyguard's attention,' he finished tactfully.

'And that's all you want me for?' she said indignantly. 'To prance around half naked so the bodyguard will look at me and forget to watch the boy?'

'You did offer to help in any way you could,' Rafe reminded her.

She gave a faint scowl. So she had. Then she stared at Rafe suspiciously.

'Are you doing this on purpose? To try and make me back out?'

'I wish you *would* back out,' he said with some feeling. 'I'd like to see you go straight back to England, and keep your nose well out of this. You're not going to do it, though, are you?'

'Definitely not,' she confirmed.

'Then you'd better get used to taking orders. As far as this operation is concerned, what I say goes. If I tell you to strip off completely, I expect you to do it. And without any arguments. Is that understood?'

'I suppose so,' Kate agreed, although there was a faintly rebellious note in her voice.

'I want a straight "yes", or I'll call the whole thing off.' Rafe's gaze held hers relentlessly. 'I'm waiting to hear it, Kate.'

'Yes,' she muttered.

He seemed satisfied with that. 'Then get yourself off to Nice and buy that bikini. And I want it to be a real eye-catcher,' he warned. 'Forget about modesty. Just go for the sexiest thing you can find.'

Kate picked up the money, and then went to collect her car keys. She was just heading out of the front entrance, automatically obeying Rafe's orders, when she suddenly stopped dead.

What on earth was she getting herself into? At the very least, they were going to trespass on someone's private property. No, not just someone. A man called Martin Foster, who apparently had enough power and influence to make life very uncomfortable for her and

Rafe if they were caught. And why? Because of a six-year-old boy whom she didn't even know—hadn't even *seen*.

Crazy, crazy, crazy! And it was all Rafe's fault. He was the one who had got her mixed up in this. She had come here for a quiet holiday, and with vague ideas about writing a novel. Now, she was mixed up with a kidnapping, and heaven knew where it would all end.

How had she got mixed up in it? Why had she ever volunteered? Was it just because of the boy? Or because her world had somehow changed rather dramatically at the moment when Rafe had kissed her?

Kate decided that she didn't even want to think about that. 'It's because of the boy,' she muttered to herself firmly, as she walked out of the door. And she kept repeating that to herself all the way to Nice.

CHAPTER FIVE

The next morning, Kate was up very early. As she paced restlessly around the villa, she tried to convince herself that she didn't feel nervous.

'There's still time to back out,' she told herself several times. 'Rafe would understand. In fact, he'd probably be pleased!'

She turned round, to find that Rafe had silently appeared in the doorway.

'How long have you been standing there, watching me?' she demanded.

'Only a few seconds,' he said easily. He came a little further into the room. 'You look pretty edgy. Want to change your mind? You don't *have* to come.'

She instantly responded to the note of challenge in his voice. 'I'm fine, and I'm coming along,' she announced firmly. 'You're not getting rid of me that easily!'

'I'm beginning to wonder if I'm ever going to get rid of you at all,' he said, in an unexpectedly reflective tone. Then his voice became brisker again. 'Are you wearing the bikini?'

'I've got it on under my dress.'

'OK, then let's go.'

The sun was shining so brightly that Kate couldn't understand why she was feeling cold. Then she realised that it was because of nerves. Agreeing to do something like this was one thing. Actually going through with it was something else again!

They got into Rafe's car, and then drove briskly away from the villa. Since it was still quite early, the traffic was fairly light. Rafe headed along the coast, finally turning off down a side road which led to a tiny bay.

No one else was around. Rafe ran the car almost down to the beach, and then parked it on a strip of grass. 'Martin Foster's villa is about half a mile along the coast,' he told her. 'We'll have to swim from here. Can you make it that far?'

'Easily,' she replied, confident about her own abilities in the water. Although, at that moment, that was about the only thing she was confident of!

Rafe got out of the car, and then began to strip off. Kate undressed rather more slowly. Finally, though, she stood there in just the bikini she had bought in Nice.

It was fuchsia-pink and *very* brief. Rafe's gaze slid over it and she saw his eyes darken appreciatively.

'Is it all right?' she enquired edgily. 'Do you like it?'

'There's very little of it to like,' he replied drily. 'You could make the whole thing out of a small handkerchief!'

'Well, I think it looks fine!' Kate snapped back defensively. 'In fact, I feel very good in it.'

'Move too fast, and you'll look good *out* of it,' Rafe commented. 'What the hell's holding it up?'

'Me!' she said, with some annoyance, '*I'm* holding it up. I'm not exactly flat-chested!'

'I'd noticed.' His mouth relaxed into the first smile of the day. 'Let's get into the water before I start noticing a few more things.'

The sea struck cool against her warm skin, but Kate was glad of that. Perhaps it would chase away the flush that had started to spread over her face!

Rafe swam smoothly and not too fast, so that she could easily keep pace with him. They kept some distance from the shore, but Kate could still see the luxurious villas that were tucked away behind the trees. This was definitely millionaires' row. They made Great-Uncle Henry's villa look like a small cottage by comparison!

After they had been swimming for a while, Rafe stopped altogether and began to tread water.

'What is it?' she asked.

'See that outcrop of rocks ahead?'

An irregular line of rocks jutted out into the sea about a hundred yards ahead of them. 'Have we got to swim round it?' asked Kate.

'Not yet. On the other side is the stretch of private beach that belongs to Martin Foster's villa.'

Kate felt a sudden quiver of nervousness deep in her stomach. 'What are we going to do?' she asked, a trifle apprehensively.

'We'll head for the rocks, and take a breather,' Rafe decided. 'Then we'll take it from there.'

They reached the rocks without any problems, and clambered out on to one that was flat and low. Kate stretched her slightly tired limbs, and then looked at Rafe. 'What now?' she asked.

''Let's take a look at Martin Foster's beach.'

Rafe climbed confidently over the rocks, while Kate followed rather more cautiously behind. In a couple of minutes, they were at the top of the outcrop, and looking down at the beach beyond.

From here, they had a perfect view. The strip of sand ran round in a wide semi-circle, backed by trees and flowering shrubs. Kate could just glimpse the villa itself, a little higher on the hillside, and she swallowed nervously.

Rafe must have seen her reaction. 'Wishing you hadn't come?' he asked perceptively.

'I've never trespassed before,' she admitted.

'We're not trespassing yet,' he told her. 'Not until we actually set foot on that beach. And we're not going to do that for a while.'

Kate relaxed a fraction. 'Then what are we going to do?' she asked. 'Just sit here?'

'Why not? This is a perfect vantage-point. There are marvellous views—in all directions,' he added with a grin, looking rather pointedly at the fuchsia-pink bikini.

'Just keep your mind on the matter in hand,' Kate instructed a little primly. 'This isn't the time for thinking about things like that!'

'It's rather difficult not to,' he admitted. 'In fact, I might have to take a dip now and then—just to cool down!'

'If I'd known you were going to get over-excited, I'd have put some bromide in your coffee this morning,' she retorted.

'Bromide?' he queried, shooting an amused glance at her.

'Isn't that what you're meant to take when you're feeling over-stimulated?' Kate enquired in a slightly acid tone.

'I believe it is,' he agreed comfortably. 'But don't worry. I'm not going to get completely out of control and jump on you. I certainly enjoy sex, but I can live without it for a while if I have to. All I'm getting is a perfectly natural reaction to being close to a gorgeous near-naked girl.'

He was making it sound as if any pretty female wouldn't have much trouble in turning him on. For some reason, Kate didn't like that.

'I thought you were meant to be very professional in your work,' she commented pointedly. 'I don't think you can be a very good private detective if you're distracted this easily!'

'But I usually work on my own,' Rafe reminded her. 'I hardly ever work with a partner—and never with a female one.'

'I don't see why that should make any difference.'

His dark eyes gleamed. 'Don't you? Then you've a lot still to learn, Kate.'

This time, Kate didn't bother to answer. She was already feeling very much on edge—she didn't need a conversation like this to make things even worse!

They sat in silence for several minutes. The sun was gradually growing hotter, and the beach remained deserted.

'How long have we got to stay here?' asked Kate at last.

Rafe shrugged. 'All day, if necessary.'

Her eyes shot wide open. 'All day? But what are we going to do to pass the time?' Then, as she saw the wicked grin that spread over his face, she gave a black scowl. 'Don't bother to answer that!'

Rafe sprawled out more comfortably on the rock. 'I suppose I should have warned you. A lot of the time, this sort of work is plain boring. Watching someone, or waiting for something to happen—and quite often it never does.'

'You mean we could sit here all day and not catch even a glimpse of the boy?'

'It's quite likely.'

'But what would we do then?'

'Come back tomorrow,' Rafe replied in an unruffled tone.

Kate groaned. 'In that case, I'm definitely going to bring a cushion. This rock already feels hard!' She shifted her position, rubbed herself ruefully and added, 'I think I need a little more natural padding.' Then, when she saw the look in Rafe's eyes, she decided it was definitely time to change the subject. She was beginning to recognise that gleam as dangerous. 'How did you get involved in this case in the first place?' she asked. 'I mean, did the boy's mother just pick you out of the phone book with a pin?'

'Not exactly.' She had the impression that Rafe was a little reluctant to add more, but eventually he went on, 'We—knew each other a few years back.'

Kate's ears instantly pricked up. 'Knew each other?' she repeated. 'How well?'

'Pretty well,' he admitted. 'For a while, we thought it might turn into something serious. Eventually, though, we found out that we were much better at being friends than lovers. Anyway, Jillie—that's the boy's mother—moved on, and eventually she met up with Martin Foster. He had money, good looks, and a whole lot of other things going for him. Jillie must have thought she'd really struck it lucky.'

'She must have been rather special herself,' Kate said slowly, as she tried to take in this unexpected revelation. Never for one moment had she suspected that Rafe had *known* the boy's mother. And apparently known her well. 'I mean, if Martin Foster's got all this money and power, he must have had his pick of dozens of women.'

'Jillie's very beautiful,' Rafe said simply, and Kate's stomach curdled with pure jealousy. She was horrified at her reaction, but she just couldn't help it. 'Just about every male who meets her falls in love with her. Martin Foster was no exception.'

'Then what went wrong?'

A darker look came over Rafe's face. 'Apparently, he just grew tired of her. Despite her looks, Jillie isn't a very sophisticated girl. She has very straightforward and simple tastes in just about everything. I suppose it was her air of innocence that first attracted Martin Foster—and which finally bored him. He's a man who apparently likes a lot of variety in his life—and in his bed.'

'So Jillie got the boot?' Despite herself, Kate couldn't help feeling a twinge of sympathy for the unknown girl.

'That's about it,' Rafe agreed tersely. 'Foster thought he wouldn't have any problems getting rid of her—and he didn't. Jillie had had more than enough by then. But he didn't count on the fact that she would take their son with her. He'd expected her to give in over that, the way she had always given in to him over everything else. But it turned out that Jillie had a tough streak that no one knew about. She was determined to keep her son, and she fought Foster every inch of the way. And in the end she won—at least, legally. So Martin Foster simply stepped outside the law, and snatched the boy away from her.'

Kate gave a small shiver. 'That must be an awful thing to happen.'

'Unless you're a mother, I don't think you can appreciate just how awful it is,' he said in a grim tone.

'And that's when Jillie turned to you?'

'She knew what line of work I was in, and so she came to see me. She was at her wits' end, almost on the verge of a complete breakdown. She kept begging me to get her child back for her.' He gave a resigned shrug. 'How could I refuse to help her?'

A beautiful girl, who was an ex-lover? Jealousy gnawed at Kate's nerve-ends again, and she forced herself to ignore it.

'Of course you had to help,' she said in a subdued tone. 'What will happen if you can't get the boy back?'

'I think it'll kill Jillie,' he said simply.

Kate chewed her bottom lip. 'We keep calling him "the boy",' she said at last, in a low voice. 'He must have a name.'

'Harry,' said Rafe, after a short pause. 'His name is Harry.' He looked at Kate. 'I saw him once. He was about—oh, ten months old. I met Jillie quite by chance, and we sat and talked for a while about old times. Harry was in his pushchair, and he kept throwing this stuffed toy out on to the grass. He thought it was a great game. Then I didn't see Jillie any more after that until she got in touch with me and pleaded with me to help her.'

Kate wondered if Rafe was still carrying a torch for the beautiful Jillie, but just didn't have the nerve to ask him.

'You don't think you might be biased in this case?' she said at last, rather hesitantly. 'I mean, you've only heard Jillie's side of the story. Martin Foster might tell a very different tale.'

'Jillie never lies about anything,' Rafe said bluntly. 'And after I'd spoken to her, I did quite a lot of research into Martin Foster's background and character. All I can say is that I wouldn't want him to bring up any child of mine. And even if he was the best father in the world—and, from all accounts, he certainly isn't—I still think Harry should be with Jillie. A child of that age needs his mother.'

'Ideally, a child should have both parents. But I suppose you're right,' agreed Kate. 'If the parents have to split up, then most kids want to stay with their mother.'

Rafe stared ahead of him. 'I was eleven years old when my parents died,' he said unexpectedly. 'I missed both of them like hell, but it was the death of my mother that really got to me. I still miss her.' He gave a lop-sided smile. 'Does that sound crazy, at my age?'

Kate swallowed hard. 'No, it doesn't.' Then she added hesitantly, 'But they were only your adoptive parents. Didn't that make any difference?'

'None at all,' he replied without hesitation. 'They were the people who had brought me up and loved me. As far as I was concerned, they were the only family I had.'

Kate was silent for quite a long while. Then she eventually said in a rather tentative voice, 'Have you ever tried to trace your real parents?'

'No,' said Rafe. 'I know that some adopted kids need to do that, and even get quite obsessive about it, but it's never been like that for me. As far as I'm concerned, my family were the people who raised me. Thanks to them, I know who I am and where I'm going. I don't want to dig up the past, and disturb a lot of other people's lives as well as my own. In my book, it's the present and the future that are important. The past is over and finished with. You can't change it, so it's best to let it be. If you start getting obsessed by it, then it can ruin your life.'

'You're a very well-balanced man, aren't you?' commented Kate, and she couldn't keep a faint note of admiration out of her voice.

Rafe raised one eyebrow gently. 'Is that a compliment?'

'I suppose so.' She looked at him curiously. 'What was it like, living with Great-Uncle Henry?' she asked. 'I mean, he was a bit odd, wasn't he?'

'Let's just say that, from the age of eleven, I didn't have a very conventional sort of upbringing,' remarked Rafe, with a wry twist of his mouth.

'I'd already gathered that. You haven't grown up to be a very conventional sort of man!' Then she looked at him reflectively. 'My mother said you didn't even go to school. Is that true?'

He shrugged. 'Not exactly. I went now and then. And Great-Uncle Henry filled in any gaps in my education. He took me round dozens of different museums and art galleries, and made me look at just about every exhibit. He knew some fascinating people, and he would invite them to the house and then let me stay up and listen while they talked about every subject under the sun. He followed politics and world affairs very closely, and made sure I understood what was going on. He had contacts in the House of Commons, the City, the Stock Exchange, and he would take me round all the different institutions, explaining exactly how they worked.' He gave a brief smile. 'I often think I had a better all-round education than anyone who regularly attended school.'

Kate was fascinated. 'I didn't know Great-Uncle Henry was like that. I thought he was just——'

'Just an eccentric?' Rafe finished for her. 'Yes, he was. But he was a very clever eccentric.'

Kate remembered some family gossip that she had accidentally overheard some time back. 'Did you know that *my* parents considered taking you in, after your parents were killed?' she asked him.

Rafe looked faintly surprised. 'No, I didn't know that.' Then his mouth curled into a slow smile. 'My guess is that it was your father's idea—and that your mother soon put a stop to it.'

'Yes, she did,' admitted Kate. 'Do you wish my father had put his foot down? That he had insisted on taking you in?'

'I fitted in very well with Great-Uncle Henry,' replied Rafe, in an unperturbed tone. Then he added drily, 'I don't think I'd have got along quite so well with your mother.'

Kate grinned. 'She always swore that when you were younger you were half child and half devil.'

'Some people might agree with her about that,' commented Rafe, with a flash of amusement. 'I did run pretty wild for quite a long while.'

'But you've grown out of it now—haven't you?' she queried, her eyebrows lifting slightly anxiously.

'Most people think that I have,' he agreed silkily.

Kate looked straight at him. 'Are you trying to make me nervous?'

'No,' he said equably. 'I'm just teasing. Can't you tell by now when I'm doing that?'

'Not always,' she admitted.

'Then in future, perhaps I'd better warn you. I don't want you to be scared of me, Kate.' There was a subtle change in his voice, and she was suddenly very aware of it. She could already feel her skin responding with a faint prickling sensation.

'How did you get to be a private investigator?' she asked rather hastily, thinking that it might be a lot safer if she kept him talking.

Rafe's eyes briefly gleamed, as if he knew perfectly well why she wanted to keep the conversation going. To her relief, though, he then began to answer her question.

'I tried various jobs, but I couldn't seem to find anything that really interested me. I suppose the up-bringing I got at Great-Uncle Henry's didn't really fit me for ordinary employment. Then I saw an adver-tisement placed by a private investigator, who was looking for an assistant. I thought, why not try it? I'd already tried just about everything else, and not found anything I enjoyed doing. I didn't really expect to like this any better, but I was wrong. I enjoyed the lack of routine, the odd hours, the even odder people I ran into. I stayed on until I'd learnt just about everything there was to learn about the business, and then I branched out on my own.'

'It's a weird job for a grown man,' Kate remarked.

'Yes, it is,' he agreed, quite unruffled by her criti-cism. 'But I like it, and most of the time I do it well. I've no plans for giving it up.'

As he finished speaking, he slid one finger very lightly down the line of her spine. Kate jumped at his touch, and then shivered as his finger kept moving.

'You're very nervy today,' he observed.

'I am not nervy,' she denied indignantly. 'I'm never nervy!' Except when I'm around you, she added silently to herself. 'I'm just—just a bit on edge,' she hedged, frantically fishing around for a plausible explanation. 'That's hardly surprising, considering why we're here.'

'You seemed quite all right until I touched you,' Rafe pointed out.

'Well, I wasn't,' Kate insisted. At the same time, she could feel an annoying flush of colour seeping into her cheeks.

'Mmm,' mused Rafe thoughtfully. 'Did you know that you look even more gorgeous than usual when you get hot and flustered?'

'Oh, stop it!' Kate retorted crossly.

He didn't answer her. Instead, to her consternation, he bent his head and kissed the side of her throat.

'Will you cut that out?' she squeaked.

'No, I don't think so,' he said, after a moment's consideration. 'I like you, Kate.' Another kiss landed at the base of her throat. 'I like you a great deal.'

The colour blazed even more brightly in her face. 'I don't know how you can even think about such things at a time like this,' she said, in a voice that was suddenly very shaky.

He gave a totally wicked grin. 'I think you should always make the most of every opportunity that presents itself.'

She opened her mouth, ready to tell him that she definitely didn't agree with him. Before she could get any words out, though, he deftly covered it with his own, so that all that came out was a muffled gurgle.

One of his hands was at her breast now, and she should have been outraged, but she wasn't. That was a little scary. She tried to free her mouth, but every time she moved her head he simply moved with her, so that the kiss just went on and on.

Rafe finally brought it to an end in his own good time. Then he raised his head and looked down at her with some satisfaction.

'I enjoyed that,' he told her. 'I didn't realise there could be such advantages, working with a female partner.'

'Well, I'm glad that *you* had a good time,' she said pointedly.

He remained infuriatingly unruffled. 'No use pretending that you hated every moment of it. I'm not exactly inexperienced in these matters.'

'I'm sure you're not,' she retaliated. 'But practice doesn't always make perfect!'

His dark gaze fixed on her gleefully. 'Want to tell me which bits weren't so good?' he invited. 'Then perhaps we could work at them, to get them right.'

'Oh, you're impossible!' she muttered. She glared back at him. 'Have you forgotten why we're here?'

'Not for a single moment. But since we've probably got to be here for a long time, don't you think this is a very nice way to pass the time?' he purred.

And the awful thing was that Kate felt an extraordinary compulsion to agree with him. It *was* nice. It was more than nice, and that was precisely why it scared her so much. This was no time for getting involved with anyone—and especially Rafe. She was quite sure that he could turn her head—and her heart—upside-down if he tried hard enough. The trouble was, would it mean anything more to him than a pleasant diversion? She doubted it. It would be far better not to get involved at all—or, at least, no more than she was right now.

And how far was that? questioned a little voice inside her head.

No more than a few kisses and a couple of caresses, she argued with herself. It definitely didn't go any deeper than that!

Rafe's hand touched her arm again. This time, though, his fingers gripped her quite hard and she realised that his mood had suddenly changed.

'Look,' he directed her attention, in a low voice. 'Someone's coming down to the beach.'

Kate found it quite an effort to remember exactly why they were here. Rafe had managed to confuse her so completely that it had driven just about everything else out of her mind. She gave a quick shake of her head, to try and clear it, and then tried to concentrate on what was happening.

As her gaze swung towards the beach, she saw two people walking across the sand. A small boy, and a very large and muscular man.

Her gaze fixed first on the smaller figure. She was too far away to see very many details, but she could make out a mop of bright blond hair, a too pale face, and rather thin arms and legs.

'Is that Harry?' she whispered.

Rafe nodded.

'Who's the gorilla with him?' Kate asked, in the same low voice. 'Is that Martin Foster?' she went on disbelievingly.

'No. My guess is that he's the bodyguard.'

Kate's eyes slid over the man's huge chest, his thick arms, massive thighs, and watchful expression. 'If he's a bodyguard, he looks as if he's very good at his job,' she remarked gloomily. 'He could probably flatten both of us with one hand before we got anywhere near the boy.'

Rafe looked along the beach in both directions, and then back towards the villa. 'Just the one body-guard,' he remarked thoughtfully.

Kate looked at him a little incredulously. 'With a gorilla like that, one is all you need!' Then she gave a resigned shrug. 'What do we do now? Give up and go home?'

'No,' Rafe said decisively. 'We'll take a swim towards the beach.'

'Fine,' she said immediately. 'You do that. I'll just stay here and watch.'

'I thought you wanted to help?'

'I do. But I forgot to tell you that I'm also a coward. That man gives me the creeps!'

'You'll be perfectly safe,' Rafe assured her. 'Nothing will happen to you. Do you think I'd let you take any risks?'

'I've no idea. The more time I spend with you, the less I think I know you!'

Unexpectedly, he smiled. 'But I know you, Kate. Since you've come this far, you won't back out now.' He lowered himself into the water. 'Let's start swimming,' he instructed. 'I'll tell you what to do as we go along.'

You're going to regret this, Kate warned herself as she flopped into the water alongside him. Then she gave a small sigh, and began swimming.

Rafe issued instructions at some length as they swam along parallel to the shore. 'Have you got it?' he said at last.

'Of course,' she said, a little indignantly. 'I'm not an idiot!'

They were quite a way out from the shore, and drawing level now with the boy and the bodyguard. Rafe and Kate both turned their heads, and then waved cheerfully at the couple on the beach. The bodyguard glared at them, and then ignored them. Harry gave a rather half-hearted wave, but then lowered his arm again as the bodyguard said something to him.

Kate kept on swimming. Anyone watching from the shore could see that she and Rafe meant to swim right round to the next bay. After she had gone about twenty yards, though, Kate gave a sudden yell and disappeared briefly under the waves. Rafe, who had been swimming a short distance ahead, immediately stopped. Kate shouted again, sounding rather panicky now, and then sank under the water for rather longer this time.

Rafe headed back towards her with long, powerful strokes, dived down and hauled her back to the surface. Then he began to head towards the shore, his hands hooked firmly under her arms as he towed her along.

As they neared the beach, the bodyguard strode towards the water's edge. 'This is private property,' he shouted at them. 'Stay away from here.'

Rafe simply ignored him. Instead, he hauled Kate out of the water, and she made a great show of holding her leg and groaning with great authenticity.

'My cousin's got cramp,' Rafe called out to the bodyguard. Then he dumped Kate on the sand, and briskly began to rub her leg.

The bodyguard came closer. As he loomed over them, Kate felt a small shiver cross her skin. He certainly was big!

'This is private property,' repeated the bodyguard. 'You'll have to leave.'

Rafe gave a slightly impatient shrug. 'We can't go yet. My cousin's got to rest for a few minutes. If she goes back into the water straight away, she'll drown.'

For the first time, the bodyguard looked rather uncertain. Then he walked away a few steps, took out a small walkie-talkie that was clipped to his belt, and spoke into it in a low voice.

'What's he doing?' whispered Kate.

'Probably asking for instructions,' replied Rafe, under his breath. 'It doesn't look as if the gorilla is very good at making decisions for himself.'

For the first time, Kate allowed herself to look at the boy. He was standing to one side, and staring at them. Kate saw that he was rather small for his age, which made him look slightly frail. She swallowed hard. He looked lost and horribly lonely. She wanted to give him a big hug and tell him that everything was going to be all right. Only she couldn't do that, because she had no idea how this was all going to turn out.

Rafe also glanced over at Harry, who was beginning to show just a little more interest in the two people who had unexpectedly turned up on his beach. 'We haven't got long,' he murmured to Kate, in a low undertone. 'Can you distract the guard for a few minutes?'

Kate wrinkled her nose. 'I suppose so. It isn't going to be much fun, though.'

'Just do your best. Remember, he can't get up to anything while I'm just a few yards away.'

'I hope you're right!' Then she got to her feet and made a great show of testing the leg in which she had pretended to have cramp. She took a few limping steps, and then turned in the direction of the guard. 'Sorry to be such a nuisance,' she said, smiling at him brightly. 'This cramp just hit me out of the blue.' She hobbled towards him, well aware that the flimsy top of her bikini was clinging wetly to her breasts, and hiding very little. She could feel the bodyguard's eyes fixed on her, and suppressed a small shiver. You're doing this for Rafe, she reminded herself. And for Harry.

Out of the corner of her eyes, she could see that Rafe had begun to move closer to Harry. The body-guard started to turn his head towards them, and Kate hurriedly let out a small squeak. At the same time, she let her leg buckle; then she made a great show of clutching the bodyguard's arm to stop herself from falling.

As her fingers closed round his thick, hairy forearm, she felt slightly sick. She took a deep breath, and somehow managed to flash another brilliant smile at him. 'Good job you were there,' she said. 'My leg just gave way again. Do you mind if I hang on to you for a few moments?'

From the look on the bodyguard's face, it was clear that he didn't mind at all. Kate briefly closed her eyes, and hoped she had the stomach to keep this up for a while longer.

She could heard the faint murmur of voices behind her, and guessed that Rafe was now talking to Harry. Unfortunately, the bodyguard suddenly became aware of it, too. He quickly shook himself free of Kate, and began to lumber towards Rafe.

'Leave the boy alone,' he instructed. 'You're not to talk to him.'

Rafe looked faintly surprised. 'I only asked his name.'

'Just leave him be.'

The first signs of annoyance began to show on Rafe's face. 'You certainly like to throw your weight around, don't you?'

'Just do as I say!' instructed the bodyguard.

'And if I don't want to do that?' Rafe challenged him.

Kate looked at Rafe uncertainly. What on earth was he up to? She couldn't tell if he was still acting, or if this was for real. She certainly hoped that he was acting. It would be sheer madness to take on that bodyguard!

The bodyguard's eyes were now gleaming, as if he relished the thought of being challenged. Kate recognised the look, and her heart sank. This was a man who enjoyed violence. Rafe had better back off pretty quickly if he didn't want to be pulverised!

But Rafe showed no sign of wanting to do any such thing. Instead, he walked a little nearer to the bodyguard; then he stared at him very coolly. 'I don't think I like your attitude,' he told him.

Kate groaned. This was suicide!

The bodyguard took a swaggering step forward. 'You and your cousin are trespassing,' he growled at Rafe. 'I ought to throw the two of you right off this property.'

'Want to try it?' invited Rafe softly.

Kate closed her eyes. She couldn't bear to look as the bodyguard's great hands began to flex. He was obviously looking forward to taking Rafe apart! She quickly opened them again, though, when she heard an odd grunting sound. To her amazement, she found

that the bodyguard was now lying on the ground, with
one arm twisted hard behind his back. And Rafe was
holding very firmly on to the other end of that arm,
keeping the bodyguard locked in a very uncomfortable position.

She remembered when Rafe had pulled that little
trick on *her*. It must be one of his favourite party
pieces! The bodyguard certainly looked very surprised. He shifted his huge weight around, and kept
grunting under his breath, but it wasn't getting him
anywhere. With just a little pressure, Rafe could keep
him exactly where he was for as long as he liked.

'Perhaps you'd like to apologise to me and my
cousin?' Rafe suggested. 'You certainly haven't been
very helpful or polite.'

The bodyguard was becoming quite purple in the
face, and his eyes glowed ferociously. It was probably
a very long time since he had been humiliated like
this.

'You want to take your time?' Rafe went on. 'That's
fine by me. I can stay here all day, if necessary.'

Until now, the confrontation between the two men
had occupied the whole of Kate's attention. Quite
suddenly, though, she realised that she was missing a
marvellous opportunity to talk to Harry without any
interference from the bodyguard.

She turned round to look for the boy, but couldn't
see him. At first, she thought he must have run back
to the villa. Perhaps he had been frightened by the
sight of the two men fighting, she thought with a flash
of guilt. She should have thought of the boy straight
away, instead of being horribly fascinated by the
struggle.

Then she glanced towards the water, and her entire nervous system abruptly went cold.

'Rafe!' she yelled. 'The boy—he's swimming out to sea!'

The small blond head was already a surprising distance from the shore. Harry must have slipped into the water almost as soon as the two men had begun their confrontation.

Rafe released his grip on the bodyguard, who immediately grabbed hold of Rafe's leg with his huge hands.

'Let go of me, you damned fool!' Rafe roared furiously. 'Do you want the boy to drown?'

The sense of what he was saying must have finally filtered through to the bodyguard, because he slowly released his grip. Rafe growled something fiercely under his breath. Then he raced down to the water's edge, plunged in, and began to swim powerfully after the small boy, who was still heading doggedly out to sea.

CHAPTER SIX

KATE could hardly bear to watch. 'Please, don't let the boy go under,' she prayed frantically beneath her breath. 'Let Rafe get there in time.'

The distance between the dark and the fair head began to steadily close. She could see that Harry was slowing down now, while Rafe was still forging ahead at the same fast speed.

She let out an audible sigh of relief as Rafe at last caught up with the boy. The two of them seemed to tread water for quite a long time; then Rafe began to head back to the beach, with the boy in tow.

'What the hell's going on here?' demanded an unfamiliar voice from just behind Kate.

She spun round, and found herself looking at a tall, middle-aged man, with powerful features that were tensed into a dark frown. Then his brows drew even closer together. 'Is that my son out there?' he asked incredulously.

Rafe and Harry had reached the shallower water now. Rafe scooped the clearly exhausted boy up into his arms, and carried him the rest of the way.

'Is he all right?' asked the tall man roughly as Rafe came towards him.

'He's fine,' replied Rafe. 'Just tired.'

'What on earth happened?'

'He swam too far out, that's all,' came Rafe's easy response. 'It's hard to judge distances when you're his age.'

The tall man visibly relaxed. 'I'm Martin Foster,' he introduced himself. 'And this is my son, Harry.' Then he turned and glared at the bodyguard. 'I pay you to make sure that nothing like this ever happens,' he said curtly.

The bodyguard started to mutter something, but Rafe cut in smoothly. 'It's so hard to get reliable staff nowadays, isn't it?' he said, in a sympathetic tone.

The bodyguard let out a strangled splutter, and Kate couldn't really blame him. After all, he couldn't have done much to stop Harry's sudden bolt for freedom. Rafe had had him in a very painful armlock at the time!

'I expect you're wondering what the two of us are doing here,' Rafe went on in the same polite tone. 'I realise that this is private property, but I'm afraid we didn't have much choice except to come ashore. My cousin and I were out for a swim, and she suddenly got hit by cramp. We had to head for the nearest beach, and it happened to be yours.' He paused for a moment. 'We did have a little trouble with your bodyguard here,' he said, in a brilliant under-statement, 'but we were just getting things settled when my cousin noticed that your boy had swum right out of his depth.'

Kate had to admire Rafe's choice of words. It wasn't exactly the truth, and yet it wasn't a complete lie.

The bodyguard was still trying to cut in, obviously bursting to tell his side of the story, but Martin Foster silenced him with one peremptory wave of his hand.

'I'm extremely grateful to you,' he said, turning to address Rafe again. 'And I'm sorry that a member of my staff should have been so obstructive and in-competent. You probably saved my son's life. That puts me completely in your debt. If there's some way I can show my gratitude——'

Kate very nearly blurted out that he could show his gratitude by returning Harry to his mother, but just managed to stop herself in time. Instead, she gave a slightly choked cough, and Martin Foster turned to look at her closely for the first time.

From the slight darkening of his eyes, she could tell that he liked what he saw. It certainly wasn't mutual, though. There was something about the coldness of his eyes, the inflexible line of his mouth, that faintly repelled her.

'Have you recovered from your attack of cramp?' he asked her courteously.

'Yes, I'm fine now,' Kate assured him.

'Obviously, you shouldn't go back into the water for a while. You must allow my chauffeur to take you home.'

Kate was about to protest that that wasn't necessary, when she caught Rafe's eye and saw him give an almost imperceptible nod.

'Thank you. That's very kind of you,' she said.

'Are you staying locally?'

'We're staying near Nice for the next couple of days,' Rafe answered casually. 'But if your chauffeur could just take us back to our car—it's parked a short distance along the coast.'

'Of course,' Martin Foster agreed at once. 'And since you're going to be in the area for the next day or two, perhaps you could have dinner with me tomorrow evening? It's the least I can do, to thank you for saving my son.' His gaze slid over to Kate. 'I do hope you will accept,' he added softly.

Kate was dying to refuse. Despite his politeness and his good looks, she didn't like Martin Foster one little bit. Quite apart from the way in which he had begun to look at her, which gave her the creeps, she couldn't believe his attitude towards Harry. Apart from his initial outburst of anger towards the bodyguard and a very brief show of concern, he had shown incredibly little emotion. Harry could have drowned, and yet he just didn't seem to be reacting at all. He hadn't even *spoken* to the boy directly.

'We'd be delighted to come to dinner,' Rafe confirmed. 'Would seven o'clock be a good time?'

'That would be fine,' replied Martin Foster. Then he turned and signalled to the bodyguard. 'Take my son up to the villa,' he ordered. 'He's to rest for a while, and then have a light meal.'

He still didn't talk to the boy directly, though, or even look at him and Harry returned the compliment by ignoring his father. Kate didn't know if Martin Foster had an incredible lack of feeling, or if he just suffered from a complete inability to communicate with his son. Whichever it was, it must make Harry's life pretty bleak. No wonder he had wanted to stay with his mother after the divorce!

She and Rafe walked up to the villa with Martin Foster. Close to, it was as impressive as Kate had expected it to be, and she guessed that he was a man who set great store by material possessions.

A couple of minutes after he had given a brief signal, a huge, shiny limousine purred its way over to them. Martin Foster opened the door for them himself, and as Kate slid inside his eyes briefly lingered on the flimsy bikini that only just covered her.

'I look forward to seeing you again tomorrow,' he said. His gaze moved over both of them, but his words were rather obviously intended for Kate.

She somehow forced herself to smile back at him. 'I'm looking forward to it, as well,' she managed to get out, in a voice that she had to strain hard to keep pleasant.

Neither she nor Rafe said a word during the short drive back to their car. She scrambled out of the limousine fairly hurriedly; then she gave a huge sigh of relief as it drove off.

'This has been one of the weirdest—and scariest!—days of my life,' she said a little shakily. 'I kept wondering if we were going to get out of there in one piece, or if Martin Foster was going to guess what we were up to, and turn nasty.' She gave a grimace. 'And my guess is that he could be very nasty indeed, if he put his mind to it.'

'He certainly can,' replied Rafe grimly. 'Do you know what he's told Harry?'

Kate shook her head.

'That his mother's dead,' Rafe said flatly, his tone dark with disgust.

'*What?*' gasped Kate in disbelief. 'But—how do you know?'

'After I swam out to Harry, we had quite a long talk before I finally brought him back to the beach.'

'I thought you seemed to be an awfully long time rescuing him.'

'I wanted to find out what had made Harry swim off like that. It turned out that it was just a spur-of-the-moment thing. Harry saw that everyone was looking the other way, and he decided to make a bolt for it.'

'Where was he going to make for?'

'He didn't even think about that,' Rafe said tersely. 'He just wanted to get away from the villa. Since I didn't have much time, I simply asked him straight out if he had been trying to get home to his mummy. His face sort of crumpled, and he said he didn't have a mummy any more. She was dead, and had gone to heaven. I asked him how he knew that, and he said his daddy had told him.' Rafe's face twisted. 'How the hell could any man do that to a six-year-old boy?' he added bitterly.

'I don't know,' Kate said, very unsteadily. 'It isn't hard to figure out *why* he did it, though. He must have thought that if Harry believed that his mother was dead, he'd be quite happy to stay with his father.'

'But Harry certainly isn't happy,' Rafe said abruptly. 'He's as miserable as hell.'

Kate swallowed hard. It still felt as if there was a giant lump in her throat, though.

'Did you—did you tell Harry that his mother is alive?' she asked. 'That she loves him, and she's trying desperately hard to get him back?'

Rafe's eyes became shadowed. 'How could I? If I'd done that, Harry would have confronted his father with the truth, and then Martin Foster would know why we're really here.' He ran his fingers restlessly through his hair. 'It's just about the hardest thing I've ever done,' he admitted. 'Keeping the truth from that boy for a while longer. Heaven knows, I wanted to tell him, but I just didn't dare risk it.'

'You can tell him as soon as you've got him out of there,' Kate said quietly.

Rafe looked at her sharply. 'Then you're agreed that we've got to try and snatch him back?'

She shrugged helplessly. 'What else can we do? I know it's not legal. I don't even know if it's moral. When a child's that unhappy, though, you can't simply walk away and pretend it's nothing to do with you.'

'It won't be easy,' Rafe warned.

'I know that.' She somehow managed a faint smile. 'You're meant to be an expert in these things, though, aren't you?'

Rafe raised one eyebrow. 'I've never done anything *quite* like this before.'

'You'll pull it off,' she said with confidence. Then her expression changed. 'Do we really have to have dinner with Martin Foster tomorrow? I don't know that I could swallow a single mouthful, having to sit near him and knowing what he's done.'

'It'll be useful if we know the layout of the interior of the villa,' Rafe replied. 'But you don't have to come, if you don't want to. I can easily go on my own.'

Kate slowly shook her head. 'No, that wouldn't be any good,' she said, with some reluctance. 'You need me to distract Martin Foster's attention. That'll give you a much better chance to have a look around.'

Rafe didn't bother to deny it. 'You certainly made an impression on him. I think the main reason he invited us was that he wanted to see you again.'

'Just don't leave us on our own together,' begged Kate, with a small shiver. 'I really don't like that man.'

'I won't leave you,' promised Rafe. He bent his head and gave her a quick, hard kiss. 'Not for a single second.'

Kate had the feeling that he wanted to say a lot more. He rather abruptly drew back again, though, and opened the car door. 'We'd better get back,' he said, in a slightly withdrawn voice. 'We've got a lot of plans to make before tomorrow.'

Kate got in beside him, careful to keep a safe distance between them. He was right, of course. They had to think of Harry, not themselves. It was unexpectedly hard to do that, though, and that worried her. It worried her a lot. Life was complicated enough right now. She found herself thinking back to the time when she had known Rafe only as a distant cousin, and found herself briefly wishing that everything could be that simple again.

Since she didn't have anything even remotely suitable to wear for dinner at Martin Foster's elegant and luxurious villa, Kate took herself off to Nice in search of an appropriate dress. She shopped very half-heartedly, because she knew that she didn't want to see Martin Foster again. Then she thought of Harry's pale, tense little face, and was disgusted with herself for being such a coward. That kid needed help, and she was going to give him as much as possible. And if it meant seeing Martin Foster a dozen times, and at close quarters, she would do it!

She finally found a dress that was suitable. It was in a shade of jade that looked just right against her dark hair and eyes. The bodice was strapless and fitted tightly, while the skirt flowed smoothly over her hips. Although not obviously sexy, it certainly drew attention to the good points of her body, and she knew that that would be useful. If Martin Foster was looking at her, then he might not notice that Rafe was taking a very close interest in the interior of the villa.

She tramped round the shops until she found high-heeled shoes and a bag to match. Then she returned to the Villa des Anges, and spent the rest of the afternoon washing her hair and coaxing it into a fall of gleaming dark curls.

By half-past six, she was as ready as she would ever be. Carefully applied make-up made her eyes look even bigger than usual, and her lashes had been stroked with mascara to make them seem even longer. Bronze blusher gave her cheeks an almost exotic outline, and her lips gleamed invitingly, their fullness emphasised with subtly coloured gloss.

She waited in the hall for Rafe, her fingers tapping together nervously. When he finally came down the stairs she glanced up at him, and then her eyebrows shot up.

It was the first time she had ever seen him in a suit and, good heavens, it certainly did things for him! Even in denims and a sweatshirt, Rafe was a pretty impressive figure. In a dark suit, crisp white shirt and bow-tie, he was positively stunning. His hair had been brushed until it gleamed, he was clean-shaven, and meticulously groomed from head to toe.

'I've never made this much effort for a man before,' he remarked drily as he saw the startled look on her face.

'Well, when you make it for women it must knock them dead!' she said with a grin.

'You don't look so bad yourself,' he murmured, his gaze sweeping over her and very obviously liking what he saw.

'Is that the best compliment you can come up with?' she demanded, raising one eyebrow.

'For the moment, yes. I've got other things on my mind right now.'

That removed the grin from her face. For just a few moments, she had managed to forget where they were going.

'Come on, then,' she said in a resigned voice. 'Let's get this over with.'

When they reached the door, though, Rafe paused for a moment and laid one hand on her arm.

'Just remember a couple of basic rules,' he warned her. 'Behave as naturally as you can, and don't do anything stupid.'

Kate looked at him a little indignantly. 'What do you think I'm going to do? Grab hold of Harry and march him out of there, right under Martin Foster's nose?'

'You might be tempted. It's no good acting on impulse, though. That isn't the way we'll get Harry out.'

'All right,' she said, in a slightly more subdued tone. 'I'll remember that. And *you* remember your promise to stick close,' she reminded him. 'Leave me alone with Martin Foster for more than a couple of minutes and I'll probably start screaming!'

'I'll take care of you,' Rafe assured her in an even tone. 'Come on, let's go.'

It was still daylight when they reached Martin Foster's villa. This time, they approached it quite legitimately, drawing the car to a halt in front of the locked gates. Tonight, there was a guard on duty. He was obviously expecting them, because he immediately opened the gates for them. Kate was a little disconcerted, though, when he immediately closed and locked the gates again as soon as they had passed through.

'I hope it's as easy to get out of this place as it is to get in,' she muttered under her breath.

Rafe heard her, and gave an unexpected grin. 'Don't worry—we can always swim for it if things begin to get sticky.'

Kate raised her eyebrows. 'Do you know how much of Great-Uncle Henry's money I had to pay for this dress? He'll probably turn in his grave if I have to leave it behind on some beach!'

Then her rather nervous chatter had to come to an end because they were drawing up in front of the villa itself. Kate got out of the car and was glad that her dress had a long skirt. Since her legs were covered, no one could see that they were trembling.

Martin Foster himself opened the front door of the villa and welcomed them in. Kate hardly heard what he was saying, though, as he ushered them through the rooms on the ground floor. She felt as if she had just walked into the lion's den, and only the fact that Rafe was right behind her stopped her from running straight out again.

The interior of the villa was every bit as impressive as Kate had expected it to be. Crystal chandeliers hung from ornate ceilings, expensive paintings covered the walls, and the furniture had been chosen with exquisite taste. Kate didn't think it was the ideal home for a six-year-old boy, though. He would be frightened to move in case he knocked over and smashed a priceless vase, scuffed the beautifully polished floors with his feet, or spilt something on one of the immaculate surfaces.

Kate turned to Martin Foster. 'Is Harry all right?' she asked. 'I suppose he's completely recovered now from his little adventure.'

'He's fine,' he replied, in a rather cool voice. 'And I've made sure that he won't do anything like that ever again.'

Kate swallowed rather hard, and decided that she didn't want to know how Martin Foster had done that. 'Where is he?' she asked, fixing a bright smile on her face. 'We were rather hoping to see him.'

'He's in bed.'

'Isn't it rather early?'

'Not at all,' Martin Foster replied. 'I've very strict rules about bedtimes. Harry is in bed by six o'clock every night. I never make any exceptions—not even when I have visitors.'

Kate was sure that he had strict rules for just about everything, which certainly wouldn't make life much fun for Harry. She was quite willing to go along with the idea that children benefited from a certain amount of discipline, but she was also convinced that it needed to be balanced with a generous amount of freedom, so they could develop their own personalities and interests. This was no time for getting into an argument with Martin Foster, though. Anyway, she could probably discuss it with him all night without changing his attitude one jot.

He led them through to the dining-room, which was as exquisitely decorated as the rest of the villa. A long, highly polished table was surrounded by high-backed, intricately carved chairs. Silver cutlery and crystal glasses had been set out, with a very professional arrangement of roses and carnations as the centre-piece. As Kate took her seat, she found the scent of the flowers rather sickly and cloying, and her heart sank still further. She really wasn't looking forward to the rest of the evening.

The food, when it came, was perfectly prepared and served. Kate became even more depressed. It was more like being in a very high-class restaurant than someone's home!

Rafe and Martin Foster spent much of the evening discussing financial matters, which really didn't interest Kate very much. Rafe seemed to be more than holding his own in the conversation, and Kate guessed that that was thanks to Great-Uncle Henry, and the solid grounding he had given Rafe in the way that the city and the big financial institutions operated.

Towards the end of the meal, Martin Foster turned to Kate and gave her a brilliant smile. Although Kate still didn't like him in the least, she was beginning to understand why Harry's mother had married him. He could exert an enormous charm when he chose to, and he had that invisible magnetism that could so often be found in very powerful men. Kate only had to remember that this was the man who had told his son that his mother was dead, though, and she had no trouble at all in resisting his efforts to charm her.

'I'm afraid we've been neglecting you,' he apologised smoothly.

'Oh—no,' she said quickly. 'I've enjoyed listening to you. It's been fascinating.' Then she put down her napkin. 'Er—I'd like to freshen up,' she went on. 'Where do I go?'

Martin Foster snapped his fingers, and the man who had served their meal with faultless expertise moved smoothly forwards. 'Parkinson will show you.'

As she got to her feet, Rafe shot her a warning look, as if to remind her of his instruction not to do anything stupid. Kate pretended not to see it, and followed Parkinson out of the room.

The cloakroom that he led her to was as impressive as the rest of the villa. Huge mirrors, comfortable chairs, gold taps, a selection of expensive soaps, and soft, fluffy towels. Kate's eyebrows rose. Rafe had told her that Martin Foster was wealthy, but the more she saw of the way he lived, the more she realised the full extent of that wealth. How much influence could a man like that wield?

This is no time to start losing your nerve, she lectured herself severely. She quickly rinsed her hands, dried them on a pastel-pink towel, and then very cautiously opened the door.

As she had hoped, Parkinson had returned to the drawing-room. No other staff seemed to be around, and Kate quietly walked to the foot of the stairs. Her legs were shaking again, but she was determined to go through with this. Rafe was stuck in the dining-room with Martin Foster, and obviously wasn't going to get a chance to look around. She was the only one with any sort of opportunity.

She already knew what she wanted to find out—which room was Harry's. The only trouble was that to do that she had to go upstairs. If she got caught, what sort of excuse could she possibly give for snooping around?

She decided not to think about it, and instead scurried up the stairs. When she reached the top, she gave a faint groan. There were at least a dozen doors leading off the main landing, with another smaller staircase leading to the side wing of the villa, where there would be yet more rooms. There just wasn't time to look inside all of them. She had already been away far too long. Another couple of minutes, and Martin Foster would definitely begin to get suspicious.

She had just begun to open the first of the doors, deciding that she would look in as many rooms as she could in the short time that she could allow herself to stay up here, when something suddenly caught her attention. It was a small pair of shoes standing outside the third door along. Kate moved forward for a closer look. Yes, they were definitely a child's shoes! Harry must have been told to leave them out every night, so that they could be cleaned and polished ready for the morning.

Relieved that it had been so easy to find out what she had wanted to know, Kate turned round and began to skip back down the stairs. Then she came to an abrupt halt as she saw Martin Foster standing at the bottom, looking up at her.

'Miss Clarendon, are you lost?' he enquired coolly.

Kate's heart thumped, and then raced. Very slowly, she went down the rest of the stairs, until she was standing level with him. Then she put on her most apologetic expression.

'No, I'm not lost,' she told him, relieved to find that her voice sounded reasonably steady. 'I have been very rude, though. I was so fascinated by your villa that I wanted to see more of it, and I went exploring on my own. I really should have asked your permission first.'

She glanced up at him from under lowered lashes, wondering if he had swallowed that story. To her relief, she found that he was smiling again.

'I'm glad you like my house,' he said softly. 'Perhaps you would like to come back at some time and see more of it—on your own?'

Kate decided that she would rather spend time with a rattlesnake. This was hardly the time to tell him that, though!

'I don't think that I can——' she began, a little edgily.

'No, I'm afraid it's quite impossible,' Rafe's voice cut in smoothly. Kate gulped with relief. She hadn't even known he was standing close by, half-hidden by the shadows. Obviously Martin Foster hadn't either, because he looked distinctly annoyed. 'We're moving on to St Tropez in the morning,' Rafe lied, in the same easy tone. 'In fact, I'm afraid we'll have to leave now, since we want to make an early start. Are you ready, Kate?'

'Oh, yes,' she said with some relief.

'Thank you for your hospitality,' Rafe said politely to Martin Foster. 'It's been a very interesting evening.'

Martin Foster's eyes flashed briefly, but there was little he could do or say. In the end, he simply took hold of Kate's hand and let his lips touch it in a light, formal kiss.

'Perhaps we'll meet again one day,' he said meaningfully.

'It isn't very likely,' Kate said, almost cheerful now that she knew she was getting out of here. She even managed not to flinch as he touched her.

Rafe shepherded her out of the door, and she gave a huge sigh of relief as it closed behind them. Now that she was out of the villa and away from Martin Foster, she could begin to relax again.

An instant later, though, Rafe's fingers closed around her arm in a painfully hard grip. 'Get into the car,' he ordered abruptly.

Kate shot a surprised look at him. 'What's the matter?'

'Into the car,' he instructed again. Kate took one look at the expression that darkened his face, and instantly obeyed.

They shot down the drive, leaving a spray of gravel behind them. The guard opened the gates for them, and Rafe sent the car shooting through. They he drove back to the Villa des Anges at a speed which Kate was sure was quite illegal.

As he finally brought the car to a skidding halt, she turned to face him indignantly. 'What's got into you?'

'Inside!' he said grimly. When she didn't immediately obey, he got out of the car, wrenched open her door, grabbed hold of her arm and hauled her out. Then she found herself being virtually frogmarched through the front door.

Once inside, she rounded on him. 'Look,' she said furiously, 'I know you can be pretty overbearing at times, but I thought we'd gone beyond all that.'

'And *I* thought I could trust you,' Rafe replied tersely.

'What do you mean by that?'

His eyes blazed down at her. 'What was the last thing I told you before we left here tonight?'

She thought back for a moment. 'Not to be stupid,' she replied at last. 'And not to do anything impulsive.'

'Then what the hell were you doing snooping around upstairs in Martin Foster's villa?' he challenged her, still glaring down at her.

'I'd have thought that was pretty obvious,' she flashed back at him defensively. 'I thought it would help if I found out which room was Harry's.'

'It *was* obvious,' he growled. 'But if it was obvious to me, then it might also have been obvious to Martin Foster.'

Kate's mouth dropped open in dismay. 'Oh,' she said in a small voice, no defiance left in her now. 'But—you don't think he suspected anything, do you? He seemed to accept my excuse about just wanting to have a look around.'

Rafe seemed to quieten down a little. 'No, I don't think he suspected anything,' he said at last. 'But you nearly blew it,' he accused, rounding on her again. 'More than that, you took risks, Kate. Right from the start, I told you I wasn't going to allow that.'

'Well, I think that what I did was perfectly justifiable, under the circumstances,' she said, lifting her head up high again. 'And I *did* find out which room is Harry's. It's the third on the left when you reach the top of the stairs.' She couldn't resist giving him a small grin of satisfaction. 'Isn't it useful to know that?'

'Yes, it's useful,' he conceded grudgingly. Then his face darkened again. 'But you take one more risk like that, and I'll send you straight back home. I won't have it, Kate. I ought to throw you over my knee and paddle your backside for what you did tonight!'

'Want to try it?' she dared him, drawing herself up to her full height and scowling at him.

'No,' he said, after an unexpectedly long pause. 'No, I don't.' His voice had begun to take on a husky note which hadn't been there a few moments ago. 'If I did, I might end up doing something very different. And this isn't the time, Kate.'

He spun round and prowled out of the room, leaving Kate standing there with a sudden fluttering in her stomach. She had already bitten off the retort that she had been about to throw after him. She didn't want to provoke him any further this evening. Whenever she thought she had got used to Rafe's moods, he would throw another one at her, and she would find out that she wasn't used to them at all. And boy, was he edgy tonight!

Since she didn't feel like facing him again, she went up to her room. She wriggled out of the jade dress, kicked off the high-heeled shoes and headed for the shower. She stood under it until the hot water had washed away the make-up, the perfume—in fact, everything that reminded her of the evening spent with Martin Foster. When she was dry again, she didn't put on a nightdress, but instead pulled on jeans and a T-shirt. She wasn't in the least sleepy, and she knew it would be quite useless to go to bed.

The room seemed hot and airless. She flung open the windows, and then went out on to the balcony. Night-scented flowers perfumed the air, a three-quarters moon hung suspended over the sea, and the trees rustled very softly in the lightest of breezes.

Kate gave a small sigh and sank down into a chair. This was all getting to be rather more than she could handle. She had come here for a holiday, and instead had got caught up in—in what? she asked herself ruefully. In the crazy plans of her crazy cousin. Her mother was right. Rafe *was* dangerous. Kate gave another sigh. And dangerous in more ways than one.

The peace of the evening finally got to her. She closed her eyes and dozed lightly for a while, only opening them again when she heard a door being opened somewhere below.

With a small frown, she peered over the balcony; then she grinned to herself. Anyone seeing her now would think she was Juliet looking for her Romeo! Then the grin slowly disappeared. Did Rafe fall into that category? She was rather afraid that he might, given half the chance. And that thought scared her quite a lot. Rafe wasn't the settling-down sort. Rafe had a beautiful ex-girlfriend called Jillie, and Kate wasn't at all sure just how much of an 'ex' she really was. Rafe could be disturbingly close or coolly distant, according to his moods. And he could *unsettle* her so easily, which put her at a distinct disadvantage.

She was still going over all the reasons why it would be a really bad idea to get involved with Rafe when she saw a dark figure moving down one of the paths.

Kate leant even further over the balcony. 'Rafe?' she called out, in a low voice.

The figure turned and looked up at her. Rafe was wearing dark jeans and a black jumper. Apart from the pale glow of his face, he blended perfectly into the shadows once he was standing still.

'I thought you'd be asleep by now,' he said, and she could hear the frown in his voice.

'How do you expect me to sleep after a night like tonight? she demanded indignantly. Then she stared at him again. 'Where are you going?'

'That doesn't concern you,' he told her bluntly.

Kate shot a suspicious look at him. 'Are you going back to Martin Foster's villa?' When he didn't answer immediately, she gave a small sigh. 'Rafe, you're insane. You'll never get near the place. It's covered with security systems.'

'In my line of work, you get to know a lot about security systems. And when you know how they work, you know how to put them out of action.'

'You'll get caught,' she said in growing alarm. 'You'll go to gaol.'

'You're such an optimist!' he remarked drily.

'Well, if you're mad enough to go, I'm coming with you,' she said with some determination. 'We'll share a cell together!'

'No.' His reply was firm and very final. When she opened her mouth ready to argue with him, he stared up at her fiercely. 'No more risks, Kate. No matter what happens, you're to stay in your room tonight.'

She glared down at him. 'And if I don't agree?'

'I'll lock you in. And in the morning, I'll put you on the first plane back to England.'

Kate could tell the difference between a bluff and a definite threat. Anyway, no one but an imbecile would argue with Rafe when he used that tone of voice.

'OK, I'll stay here,' she said rather sulkily.

'Promise, Kate?' he pushed her.

'I said I will! Why do I have to give childish promises?'

'Because I want to hear you say it,' Rafe said implacably.

'Oh, all right,' she retorted crossly. 'I promise.'

He seemed satisfied with that. 'I'll be back before first light. Don't worry, everything will be fine.'

Rafe disappeared into the darkness, and Kate sat down before her suddenly shaky legs collapsed under her. What was he up to now? Really, the strain of living with Rafe was having a distinctly debilitating effect on her nervous system!

She spent the next couple of hours either peering out of the window, or pacing restlessly up and down. She told herself that it was daft to worry about him, that he would be fine; Rafe was well-used to looking after himself. All the same, when she finally heard his car pulling up outside, she let out an enormous sigh of relief. She skipped downstairs to meet him, and reached the hall just as the front door began to open.

Rafe came in first, but he wasn't on his own. Beside him was a small figure, dressed in pyjamas and looking decidedly sleepy. It was Harry—Rafe had gone right ahead and snatched the boy!

'Kate, you know Harry, don't you?' Rafe said calmly. 'Harry, do you remember Kate? You saw her at the beach, a couple of days ago.'

'I remember,' said Harry, giving an enormous yawn. 'Hello.'

'Hello, Harry,' Kate said in a stunned voice.

'I'm coming to stay for a few days,' Harry informed her. 'Then I'm going home to my mummy.' He yawned again, and looked up at Rafe. 'Can I go to bed now?'

'Of course you can,' replied Rafe, with a grin. He scooped the boy up into his arms, and headed for the stairs. As he passed Kate, he paused for a moment and gave her a quick kiss on the cheek. 'Coming up to bed?' he asked, with a wicked flash from his eyes.

Kate blinked a couple of times, and couldn't quite decide if she was dreaming this or not. Then she slowly trailed up the stairs after Rafe and the sleepy Harry.

CHAPTER SEVEN

THEY tucked Harry safely up in bed, with a small lamp left on beside him in case he woke up in the dark and was afraid. Then Kate collared Rafe and marched him into the next room.

'Why didn't you tell me you were going to bring Harry here tonight?' she demanded.

'I didn't know that I was,' Rafe replied in an unruffled tone. 'I set out with the idea of seeing how close I could get to the villa. It was all a lot easier than I'd expected, though—Martin Foster must be so confident that no one can touch him that he only bothers with minimal security at night. I actually managed to get right into Harry's bedroom without being seen. Harry remembered me right away—in fact, he seemed quite pleased to see me. We had a long talk, and I explained a lot of things to him—at least, as much as you can tell a six-year-old without going into too many sordid details. That kid's face when I told him his mother was still alive . . .' Rafe said, shaking his head. 'It was worth all the hassle just to see it. Anyway, I asked Harry if he wanted to come with me, and the answer was a very definite yes. He hates it at that villa, and he seems scared to death of his father.'

'What do we do now?' asked Kate a little dazedly.

'We'll both get a couple of hours' sleep. Then, first thing in the morning, I'll phone Jillie and tell her that Harry's with us, and that she can fly out and collect him whenever she likes.' He gave a broad grin. 'My guess is that she'll be on a plane as soon as she's put down the phone!'

'Then it's nearly all over?' asked Kate, with some relief. 'All we've got to do is sit and wait for Jillie to come and pick up Harry?'

'That's all,' agreed Rafe. His eyes sparkled. 'Then we're free to spend the rest of the summer doing whatever we please.'

And he looked as if he knew perfectly well what would please him right now. Kate felt a familiar twinge along all her nerve-ends. What did *she* want to do? She didn't know, wasn't sure. Everything had happened a little too fast over the last few days, and now Rafe was pressuring her into taking yet another step into the unknown.

Rafe looked at her reflectively. 'I thought we wanted the same thing, Kate,' he said, obviously seeing her uncertainty.

'Do we?' she said a little guardedly.

'Oh, yes,' he confirmed with complete assurance. His fingers gently touched her bare arm. 'We're very compatible, Kate. It's about the last thing I ever expected, but it's useless to ignore it.'

But Kate wasn't sure that being 'compatible' was enough. At least, not for her. And Rafe didn't seem to be offering anything more, not at the moment.

With a small shiver, she moved her arm away. 'Harry's in the next room,' she reminded him in a rather taut voice.

'Harry is very soundly asleep.' Rafe's dark gaze suddenly blazed down at her. 'But I'm not,' he said huskily. He bent his head, and his mouth crushed hers for a few head-spinning moments. 'And I don't think

you are, either,' came his soft challenge, as his lips
released hers again.

Kate gulped. It really wasn't fair, she thought with
just a touch of resentment. Some men kissed you, and
it didn't do a thing for you. You might just as well
have been kissing a wet flannel! Then someone else
came along, and just one brief touch could produce
the most amazing fireworks. It was baffling and very
alarming, because you never knew who that person
was going to be. And when it turned out to be
someone like Rafe...

'Still having trouble making up your mind?' he
questioned her throatily. 'That's not like you, Kate.
You're usually so decisive.' Then he grinned. 'I'd
enjoy trying to persuade you.'

His hand moved back to her arm, and rested there
for a moment. When she didn't immediately pull away,
he let his fingers drift gently up to her shoulder, and
then down, over the soft swell of her breast, leaving
small trails of fire in their wake.

Kate gritted her teeth. 'No,' she said firmly. 'This
isn't right. Not with Harry in the house.'

Rafe seemed regretful, but not particularly perturbed. 'Harry won't be around for more than a day
or two,' he reminded her. 'What excuse will you use
then?'

Kate didn't know. She decided she would worry
about it when it happened, though. Right now, she
just wanted to get out of here—before she changed
her mind!

'I'm going to sleep in Harry's room,' she told him.
'He might get scared when he wakes up and finds
himself in a strange house.'

'Coward,' Rafe taunted her gently. Then he grinned again. 'All right, run off and take refuge in Harry's room. But just remember, Harry won't be there forever. And then you're going to have to make up your mind in which direction you want to go, Kate.'

Kate scuttled rather quickly out of the room. She couldn't remember when she had last felt this disturbed and uncertain.

The sight of Harry, sprawled out in bed fast asleep, calmed her down quite a lot. She stood there for a long while, just looking at him. She had had a lot of doubts about this whole mad venture, but she was convinced now that they had done the right thing. Harry already looked a lot more relaxed and happy, and surely that was what really counted in the end?

She made herself as comfortable as she could in the chair, closed her eyes, and eventually managed to fall asleep.

She was woken up some time later by someone tugging rather urgently at her sleeve. Kate blinked blearily as she stared at the small boy standing beside her. Harry, she thought sleepily. Then her eyes shot wide open and she quickly sat up as she remembered what had happened last night. Harry! Here at the Villa des Anges.

He gave another tug at her sleeve. 'I want to go to the bathroom,' he announced. 'And I don't know where it is.'

Kate scrambled to her feet. 'Come on. I'll show you.'

Harry trotted after her as she went down the corridor and then opened the door for him. Kate tactfully waited outside, and when he came out again she took him back to the bedroom.

'Did you bring any clothes with you?' she asked.

'Yes,' he nodded. Then he pointed to a chair. 'They're over there.'

Kate sorted through the untidy bundle, and guessed that Rafe had just grabbed a couple of handfuls of everything. There was more than enough to see Harry through the next day or so, though. Rafe had brought T-shirts and shorts, undies and socks, a spare pair of sneakers, a pair of jeans and a couple of jumpers. They were all fairly crumpled, but Kate guessed that Harry wouldn't mind too much about that. And she could iron a couple of things for him, so he would look smart when it was finally time for him to meet his mother.

Harry fished out the jeans and a bright T-shirt. Then, with the natural lack of modesty of a young child, he wriggled out of his pyjamas and began to pull on his clothes.

'I bet you're hungry,' said Kate. 'What do you usually have for breakfast?'

Harry's head popped out through the neck of his T-shirt, and he looked at her with an unenthusiastic expression.

'A boiled egg,' he said, screwing up his nose.

Kate's eyebrows rose. 'Every morning?' she asked.

'Every morning,' Harry confirmed gloomily. 'They're meant to be good for me.'

'They might be good for you, but they're not very exciting,' commented Kate. 'What would you *like* for breakfast?'

His face began to brighten. 'Anything at all?'

'As long as we've got it in the cupboard.'

Harry only needed to think about it for a few moments. 'Sausages and beans,' he announced. 'And custard.'

'Not together, I hope,' Kate said faintly.

He grinned, the first real smile she had ever seen from him. 'Of course not. First, the sausages and beans. *Then* the custard.'

'Well, we'd better go down to the kitchen and see what we can come up with,' she said, with an answering grin.

When they walked into the kitchen, they found that Rafe had already got there before them, and was sitting at the table, drinking coffee.

'I thought I'd let the two of you have a lie-in,' he said cheerfully. 'Did you sleep well, Harry?'

'Yes, thank you.' Harry wandered around the kitchen, peering inquisitively around him. 'Have you got a swimming-pool?' he asked a couple of minutes later. 'Can I go swimming after breakfast?'

'I don't see why not,' said Rafe.

'I don't remember seeing any swimming-trunks among those clothes you brought,' commented Kate.

'That doesn't matter,' Harry said practically. 'I don't *have* to wear any, do I?'

'No, you don't,' said Rafe, quickly hiding a smile. 'Although, if you wanted to, you could wear a pair of underpants. They're as good as swimming-trunks.'

'I don't think I'll bother,' Harry said unconcernedly, and Kate rather hurriedly smothered a chuckle.

She sorted through the fridge and found some sausages. Then a search of the cupboards finally yielded a tin of beans. That was it, though, and she turned to Harry with an apologetic shrug.

'Sorry,' she said. 'No custard.'

'Custard?' repeated Rafe, one eyebrow shooting up.

'Custard,' confirmed Kate. 'I'll have to get some when I next go shopping.'

'It doesn't matter,' said Harry, not particularly perturbed. 'I'll have it at some other time.'

Kate cooked the sausages and heated through the beans. Then, as Harry began to tuck in, she walked over to Rafe.

'He almost seems to have forgotten everything that's happened these last few weeks,' she said in a low voice.

'Kids of his age get over things remarkably quickly,' Rafe replied. 'Once they're out of a bad situation, they just put it out of their minds and get on with their lives. And Harry seems to be very well-adjusted, with no basic emotional problems. Jillie's done a really good job of raising him.'

'Have you phoned her yet?'

'No. I wanted to see Harry first, and make sure he'd settled in all right. I'll go and ring her now. The sooner she comes and collects him, the better it will be for everybody—especially Harry.'

Rafe disappeared out of the kitchen while Harry finished his breakfast. He was gone for quite some time, and when he finally returned there was a very different expression on his face. The cheerful smile had completely disappeared, and in its place was a dark frown.

'What is it?' asked Kate in a soft murmur.

'I'll tell you later,' he replied shortly. 'When Harry's not around.'

'Can I go swimming now?' asked Harry, pushing away his empty plate.

'I think you'd better let that breakfast go down first,' answered Rafe.

Harry looked disappointed. 'How long will that take?'

'About half an hour, I should think.' Rafe held out his hand to the boy. 'While we're waiting, let's go and find the cats and give them their breakfast.'

'Cats?' repeated Harry, visibly brightening. 'How many?'

'Three,' Rafe told him. 'And perhaps you can think of some names for them. They haven't got any yet.'

They went out on to the terrace, and Kate edgily gathered up Harry's breakfast things. What had gone wrong? From the look on Rafe's face, it was pretty clear that there had been some hitch in their plans. She found that her hands were shaking slightly. Please let this turn out right, she prayed silently under her breath. Harry seemed so happy at the moment, now that he was free of his father's influence and about to be reunited with his mother. It would be really cruel if it all fell apart for him.

It was nearly an hour before she got a chance to talk to Rafe on his own. Harry was in the swimming-pool by then, while she and Rafe sat on sun-loungers and watched him, to make sure he didn't come to any harm.

'All right, what's up?' Kate asked with a worried frown. When he didn't answer straight away, she gave a frustrated sigh. 'Rafe, *tell* me! What did Harry's mother say?'

Rafe's dark brows drew together. 'I didn't speak to Jillie. It turns out that she's in hospital.'

'In hospital?' squeaked Kate. 'Why?'

'She's had to have her appendix out,' replied Rafe briefly. He still looked rather tense. 'When I last saw her, she told me she'd been getting stomach pains. She thought it was because of all the tension. It was obviously appendicitis, though.'

'Is she all right?'

'Fine, according to her mother. That's who I spoke to on the phone. It'll be at least a week before she's fit enough to come and collect Harry, though.'

'Can't Jillie's mother have Harry until she's well again? She is his grandmother, and Harry would probably be perfectly happy with her.'

'Yes, he would,' agreed Rafe. 'But Jillie's mother suffers from bad arthritis. She's confined to a wheel-chair much of the time. She couldn't possibly cope with a lively boy like Harry.'

Kate looked at Rafe suspiciously. 'What exactly does all this mean?'

'I'd have thought that was pretty obvious,' he replied evenly. 'It means that Harry's going to have to stay with us until Jillie's well enough to have him back again.'

Kate groaned; then she looked slightly apologetic. 'It isn't that I don't like having Harry here. I do. In fact, I'm really fond of him already. But right now you and I are kidnappers. That makes me rather nervous!'

'I know,' agreed Rafe. 'That's why I think it's time you went back home, Kate.'

At that, she lifted her head rather indignantly. 'And leave you and Harry here, on your own?'

'You just said you were nervous about the situation,' he pointed out. 'I'm telling you there's no need to be. Your part in this is finished. You can go back to your parents and forget about it.'

'*Forget* it?' she repeated incredulously. 'How could I ever forget either of you?'

A faint smile touched the corners of Rafe's mouth. 'It's nice to know we're so memorable!' Then his features became more serious again. 'But I want you out of this. I should never have let you stay in the first place. Heaven knows why I did. This isn't your line of work, and I must have been a little crazy to let you take the risks you did. It's over now, though. I can cope with the rest on my own quite easily. Harry and I will stay here until Jillie's fully recovered. Then I'll hand him over, and that will be it.'

'No,' said Kate flatly. 'If you're staying, then so am I. Harry needs a woman around, and——'

She stopped rather abruptly, and Rafe looked at her quizzically.

'And so do I?' he finished for her. 'Perhaps I do, Kate, but I can manage without you for a few days. It's time for you to go.'

'I'm not leaving, and that's that,' she told him in a firm voice. 'You're right, I *am* scared, but I can cope with it. Between us, we'll take good care of Harry until he can go back home to his mother.'

Rafe just looked at her for a long time. 'You're as crazy as I am,' he said at last. 'I suppose I ought to cut the arguments, and just boot you straight out of here.'

'But you're not going to?' she said hopefully.

He gave a resigned shrug. 'You're old enough—and intelligent enough—to make your own decisions. Anyway...'

'Anyway, what?' Kate prompted softly.

'I like having you around,' he admitted.

Harry's head popped out of the pool at that moment. 'Are you coming in?' he asked.

'In just a little while,' Rafe told him. 'There's something we've got to tell you first. Come out of the water for a couple of minutes—it won't take long,' he added, as Harry began to look disappointed.

He sat Harry down on the sun-lounger beside him, and then gently explained to the boy why he couldn't go back to his mother for a few days yet. Harry's face fell, and his eyes became suspiciously bright.

'Does my mummy know where I am?' he asked in a small voice.

'Yes, she does,' Rafe assured him at once. 'And as soon as she's feeling better, she's going to come and get you, and take you back home.'

Harry still looked very downcast. 'How many days before she comes?' he asked.

'Not very many,' Kate said. 'Look, I've got a calendar upstairs. Each night before you go to bed we'll mark off a day, and then you'll know when it's getting near the time for your mummy to come.'

'And in a couple of days, when she's feeling better, you can talk to her on the telephone,' Rafe added.

Harry began to brighten up just a fraction. 'I can tell her about the cats. And how well I can swim.' Then he looked rather anxious again. 'Can I stay with you until she comes? I won't have to go—anywhere else?'

Kate knew what he was telling them. That he didn't want to go back to his father's house.

'Of course you can stay with us,' she said gently. 'We really like having you here.'

Harry gave a broad smile. 'Good. Can I go back in the water now?'

As soon as Rafe nodded, he hurled himself back into the pool, sending sprays of water all over them. Kate wiped the drips from her arms, and then gave Rafe a rueful smile.

'It looks as if we're all going to be staying for the next few days,' she said.

'Yes, it does,' agreed Rafe, with a brief flash of his eyes. 'You do know what you're getting into, Kate?'

'Of course,' she said lightly. 'I'm aiding and abetting a kidnapper.'

She knew that Rafe had meant very much more than that, but she chose to deliberately misunderstand his words. She was sure that she wanted to help Harry, but she was still confused and uncertain about the rest of it—about Rafe, himself...

It'll sort itself out in time, she told herself comfortingly. And in the meantime, you don't even have to think about it. Just concentrate on looking after Harry.

The next few days passed with remarkably few problems. Harry settled in with them quite happily, and Kate was amazed that his traumatic experiences had left so few scars. He didn't even look like the same pale, tense boy they had seen on the beach on their first visit to Martin Foster's villa. His eyes were bright, he was eating like a horse, and was full of energy.

Rafe had laid only one restriction on him, which was that he was to remain either inside the villa or very close to it at all times.

'Martin Foster's going to have a lot of people looking for him,' he told Kate in a quiet voice. 'We can't risk having Harry seen by one of them.'

'Perhaps we ought to go back to England?' Kate suggested, a little uneasily.

'I don't have a passport for Harry,' Rafe replied. 'Jillie's going to bring all the necessary papers when she comes. Anyway, I think we're as safe here as anywhere.'

'But Martin Foster's only a few miles down the coast,' Kate reminded him.

'Often the best place to hide is right under someone's nose. It's the one place they hardly ever look.'

Kate fervently hoped that he was right. She was beginning to feel a lot more relaxed now, though, as the days began to pass and nothing alarming happened. Harry had spoken to his mother on the phone, which had cheered him up enormously, and every night they crossed off another square on the calendar, so he could see how long it would be before he would be going home.

At the end of the first week, Kate suggested to Rafe that it would be good for Harry to have a day away from the villa.

'He's been very good,' she explained, 'but I think he's beginning to get bored. He's spent so much time in the pool that he's starting to look like a prune, he's teased the cats so much that they've left home, and I don't think I can face another board game. We've played them all for hours!'

Rafe frowned. 'I'd rather he stayed here.'

'I know. But I thought a day at the beach wouldn't be too risky. If we choose somewhere packed with holiday-makers, surely no one will notice us?' she said persuasively. 'You know what the beaches are like—bodies packed in like sardines, and kids running around all over the place. We'd just get lost in the crowd. And it really would be good for Harry if he could pal up with some kids for the day.'

Rafe looked as if he still didn't like the idea, but he didn't actually veto it altogether. The next morning, he walked into the kitchen and looked at Kate with a touch of resignation.

'I suppose Cannes would be crowded enough,' he said. 'The three of us should be able to get lost there quite easily.'

'Cannes? Great!' grinned Kate. 'Come on, Harry, shovel down the rest of your breakfast. We're off to the beach for the day!'

'I've finished,' Harry said promptly, quickly choking down his last piece of sausage.

'Then go and get a towel and a pair of trunks—oh, hang on, you haven't got any trunks, have you?' remembered Kate. 'Well, it doesn't matter. A lot of people at Cannes don't bother with swimsuits.'

Rafe shot a severe look at her. 'I expect *you* to bother,' he told her.

'Spoilsport!' she shot back at him. Then she got up and quickly began to clear the table.

As they clambered into the car, the sunshine was hot and golden, and it promised to be a perfect day. When they reached the coast road, Rafe seemed to relax as he saw how much traffic there was around. Kate was relieved, as well. She was sure that no one would be able to pick them out in this constant stream of cars.

When they eventually reached Cannes, they cruised along the sea front for a while. As Kate had predicted, the beach was covered with tanned and virtually naked bodies. Trees and palms lined the promenade, giving it a faintly tropical air, and behind it rose the luxurious and expensive hotels where the rich and famous stayed. Elegant yachts and motorboats packed the marina, and there seemed to be more gorgeous girls here than anywhere else along the coast.

Rafe noticed Kate looking at them. 'They're probably hoping to catch the eye of some passing millionaire,' he remarked. 'If you're looking for money, this is the place to come.'

'Well, thanks to Great-Uncle Henry, *we're* not exactly poor,' Kate reminded him.

'Maybe not. But we're certainly not in the same league as a lot of these people.'

Just then, Kate's head whipped round. 'Did you see who that was?' she said a little breathlessly. 'I saw her on television just a few weeks ago!'

'Well-known faces are two a penny around here,' replied Rafe, in an unimpressed tone.

Slightly annoyed by his blasé attitude, Kate slumped back in her seat and didn't say a single word when she saw a world-famous film star saunter by.

They finally managed to find a parking space, and then trooped down to the beach. Harry raced on ahead, obviously delighted to be free of the confines of the villa. Kate watched him fondly.

'I'm really going to miss him when it's time to hand him back to his mother,' she admitted.

'So am I.' Rafe looked at her. 'You like kids?'

'Yes. Do you?'

'They've got a habit of growing on you,' he said wryly. Then he quickened his pace. 'Let's get a move on, or Harry's going to leave us miles behind.'

Ten minutes later, Kate was stretched out on the sand, with a giant parasol overhead to shade her from the fierce rays of the sun. She gave a small sigh of contentment. 'This is great,' she said dreamily.

Rafe was sitting beside her, but definitely not looking quite so relaxed.

'I didn't know you were going to wear that bikini again,' he growled, with a quick glance at the fuchsia-pink bikini which she had bought in Nice and, on impulse, had slipped on this morning.

She looked at him demurely. 'I was only following your instructions. *You* were the one who said I had to wear a swimsuit. Remember?'

'Two scraps of material like that hardly count as a swimsuit. I expected you to wear something decent.'

Kate glanced down at herself. 'This looks perfectly decent to me. It covers everything that it's meant to cover.'

Rafe's dark brows drew together. 'Only just!'

'You're lucky I'm wearing anything at all,' she told him, at the same time batting her long eyelashes at him provocatively. 'I did consider going topless. After all, hardly anyone around here seems to bother with bikini tops. And a lot have discarded the bottoms, as well,' she pointed out.

Rafe flung a brooding look at her. 'So, what stopped you?'

'I didn't want to be a bad influence on Harry,' Kate replied modestly. The grunt that Rafe gave was fairly hard to interpret, and she stifled a grin. Then she went on in the same innocent tone, 'Of course, it's not a very *secure* bikini. It's only held together with a couple of small bows. I do hope I tied them tightly enough,' she said thoughtfully. 'If they work loose—or someone gives them a gentle tug—it could just fall apart.'

Rafe muttered something under his breath that she couldn't quite catch. Then he got to his feet. 'I'm going for a swim,' he said roughly, and he rather quickly strode off down the beach.

This time, Kate allowed the broad grin to spread right across her face. She knew that she was flirting with Rafe quite outrageously, and she was amazed to find how much she was enjoying it. And she wasn't bothered about the consequences. She was perfectly safe, sitting here on this crowded beach.

While Rafe was swimming, she kept an eye on Harry. He had already made friends with a couple of boys of his own age, and they were playing football near the water's edge. Kate sat back and relaxed. She had the feeling that this was going to be a really good day.

The three of them had lunch at an open-air café, and then returned to the beach for the rest of the afternoon. Harry soon found his friends again, and was obviously having a perfectly marvellous time. Rafe, on the other hand, seemed to be getting increasingly restless, especially after Kate had been for a swim and came back to sit beside him with the pink bikini soaking wet, and clinging to her like a second skin.

By late afternoon, it was clear that Harry was at last running out of steam. He gave a couple of huge yawns, and didn't make any real objections when Rafe decided that it was time for them to return to the villa.

He fell asleep during the drive back, and when they reached the Villa des Anges, Rafe picked him up and carried him inside.

'I'll take him straight up to bed,' he said. 'My guess is that he won't wake up again until tomorrow morning.'

Kate smoothed Harry's tousled blond hair. 'He's had a great day,' she said. 'Can we do it again?'

Rafe reluctantly shook his head. 'It's too risky. I think we'd better stick close to the villa from now on. We don't want anything to go wrong at the last moment.'

He went upstairs with the boy, and Kate slowly trailed after them. She felt rather languid after all that sun and fresh air, and as Rafe took Harry to his bedroom she wandered into her own room.

Once inside, she stripped off her shorts and T-shirt, and then untied the bows on the bikini. Her skin was salty from swimming, and she decided to have a shower. She pulled on a light bathrobe, and then yawned. Like Harry, she was really sleepy. She might have half an hour's nap before she showered and dressed, ready for dinner.

The sound of the bedroom door opening made her heavy eyes fly wide open again. Then she gave a small sigh of relief as she saw it was Rafe.

'I wish you wouldn't do that,' she told him. 'It makes me really jumpy.' Then she frowned. 'Is everything all right? Harry's OK, isn't he?'

'Harry's fine,' replied Rafe, closing the door behind him and coming further into the room. 'He's still very soundly asleep.'

Kate's nerves prickled with the first intimations of alarm. 'Then what are you doing here?' she asked edgily.

'Because I'm *not* so fine. And I think you know why.'

'Do I?' she countered in a wary tone.

'Oh, yes,' Rafe told her softly. He took another step closer. 'You've had a lot of fun today, haven't you, Kate? Winding me up, and knowing that I couldn't do a damn thing about it?'

She wanted to deny it, but it was rather hard when she knew perfectly well that it was true. She didn't know *why* she had done it, though. All she knew was that she was definitely beginning to regret it—although she had the uncomfortable feeling that it was rather too late for that.

'What——' She swallowed hard, and tried again. 'What are you going to do?'

Rafe's face relaxed into a slow smile that made her stomach flip over. 'What am I going to do?' he echoed, looking at her thoughtfully. 'Well, for a start, I think that it's my turn to have some of the fun.'

His tone was lazy, but his movements were quick and much more purposeful. Kate scarcely had time to blink before he had closed the gap between them and bent his head towards hers.

His first kiss wasn't too hard or too fierce, but it still stopped her from saying anything. And when his mouth finally released hers, she couldn't even remember what words she had been trying to get out.

She was just reassuring herself that it hadn't been too bad, that she could cope with this situation quite well and hadn't found it *too* disturbing, when Rafe embarked on his second kiss.

This one was definitely different—and in just about every way! His lips demanded a response, and then reacted immediately when they got it. By the time the kiss was finally over, Kate felt as if she hadn't been left with a single scrap of privacy. His lips and tongue had explored so thoroughly that she felt completely drained, as if she had just given part of herself to him.

She tried to console herself with the fact that she was still on her feet, with her legs holding steady—although only just! She had to admit that that last kiss had definitely been a bit of a knee-trembler. She had somehow got through it, though, and she supposed that Rafe would be satisfied now.

'Going somewhere?' he enquired as she tried to pull away from him.

'But I thought——' she began, apprehension creeping into her voice.

'Thought what, Kate?' he asked silkily.

'Well, that you...' She gave an audible gulp. 'That you just wanted a kiss,' she finished, in a bit of a rush.

'I think I'd like a little more than that,' Rafe told her, his eyes gleaming brightly now.

His hands moved towards her, and easily slid open her bathrobe. Kate hurriedly tried to close it again, but Rafe caught hold of her wrists and held them away from her body; then his gaze slid over her, darkening with pleasure as he drank in the details.

'I thought I knew exactly what you looked like,' he murmured at last, 'but that bikini did hide a few secrets. For instance, I didn't know that your nipples were pale pink. Very pretty,' he said huskily. 'Almost childish—although there's definitely nothing immature about the rest of you, Kate.'

Kate's face was flaring bright scarlet by now. Rafe looked at her with a first touch of surprise. 'You're not shy, are you? Not with me?'

'Of course not,' she muttered, quite untruthfully. 'I'm just a bit—confused,' she finished evasively.

'Then let's see if I can confuse you some more,' he said with a slow smile.

His hands left her wrists and slid inside the bathrobe. Kate gave a small gasp of surprise, but then stood quite still as his hands began to move expertly over her.

'Like that?' he prompted. Then his smile deepened. 'There's no need to answer. I can see—and feel!— that you do.'

Kate was alarmed that he could read her so easily. And she was even more alarmed when, a moment later, he bent his head. She actually squeaked out loud as his tongue curled round the tip of her breast.

Rafe wrinkled his nose. 'Salty,' he commented. 'I'd prefer to lick you after you've had a shower.'

'I don't think I want to be licked at all,' she somehow got out in a distinctly shaky voice.

'Why not? It can be very, *very* nice,' he purred. 'I'd like to show you, but I'd probably end up with a raging thirst—in more ways than one,' he finished ruefully.

His fingers moved rather restlessly again, and Kate jumped.

'I think—I think you ought to stop that,' she gulped.

'In just a moment,' Rafe promised, and there was a new huskiness threading its way through his voice now. His hand skimmed lower, and a wave of pleasure echoed through Kate's body. Instinctively she leaned towards him, and he gave a murmur of satisfaction. Then he shifted a little restlessly.

'Want to touch me, Kate?' he invited softly.

She curled her fingers into tight fists, to stop them giving in to the overwhelming impulse to do exactly as he had suggested.

'Harry might wake up——' she began defensively.

'It would take an earthquake to wake Harry.'

'He might have a bad dream,' she insisted. 'I ought to be there, in case he needs me.'

Rafe immediately released her. 'Then run away, if you want to. But remember that you can't keep running forever, Kate.' His eyes narrowed thoughtfully. 'I wish I knew why you're scared of me. Is it because I don't fit into any comfortable category? Or have you been listening to too many of those stories that the family like to tell about me?'

But Kate couldn't give him any answer. She just knew that she wasn't sure; she wasn't quite ready.

Rafe correctly read the expression on her face. 'All right, let's leave it for now,' he said in a frustrated voice. 'But when you've stopped running, Kate—I'll be waiting for you.'

He wheeled round and rather quickly left the bedroom. Kate wanted to run after him and ask him to come back, but she didn't. Instead, she stood in the middle of the room and trembled slightly. She hadn't expected this to happen, not with Rafe. She wished she didn't feel so uncertain of herself—so uncertain of *him*. He was older than she was, so much more experienced—and there was the beautiful Jillie hovering somewhere in the background. Did she still figure in Rafe's life? Kate didn't know, and she didn't have the nerve to ask.

It was unlike her to be so hesitant and unsure of everything. Usually she just bounced through life, knowing exactly where she was going and what she wanted.

Slowly, she made her way along to Harry's room, still trying to work it all out. Harry was still soundly asleep, and didn't stir as she stood looking at him. With his blond hair and fine features, he looked like an angel. Then Kate gave a rueful smile. He certainly wasn't very angelic when he was awake!

She dropped a light kiss on his forehead, and then curled up in the chair on the far side of the room. When she finally fell asleep, though, she dreamt of Rafe, and moved around restlessly for much of the night.

CHAPTER EIGHT

IN THE morning, Kate's head felt much clearer, but she still couldn't seem to make any decisions about Rafe. In the end, she decided to stop thinking about it until this business with Harry was finally over. It was Harry who needed all her attention during the next few days. Her own problems could wait.

Rafe shot her an enigmatic look as she walked into the kitchen, but didn't say anything about the night before, for which she was grateful.

'We're running short of several things,' he told her. 'I'll drive into Nice this morning, and pick up what we need.'

'Want me to go?' she offered.

'No, that's OK. You stay here with Harry. I won't be more than a couple of hours.'

Harry wandered into the kitchen at that point, still looking half asleep. 'Are we going back to the beach today?' he asked hopefully.

'I'm afraid not,' answered Rafe. 'But you can swim in the pool.'

'After you've had a bath and eaten breakfast,' Kate added firmly.

Harry wrinkled his nose. 'A bath?' he said without enthusiasm.

'You're still covered with salt from yesterday,' Kate told him. 'You must have spent half the day in the sea.'

'It'll wash off in the swimming-pool,' Harry said optimistically.

Rafe grinned at him. 'Nice try, Harry, but I'm afraid it won't work. Go and run the water, while Kate gets your breakfast.'

Harry trudged out of the kitchen again with a resigned look on his face, and Rafe got to his feet. 'I'd better make a start. If I leave now, I'll be back before lunch. Anything you need?'

'I don't think so. Oh, except for some more sausages,' she added. 'Harry seems to eat them by the yard!'

The rest of the morning passed pleasantly. Harry came down to breakfast looking squeaky clean, and then completely cleared his plate. Since he couldn't swim straight away after eating, he and Kate sat on the terrace for a while and played Monopoly. As always, Kate was surprised at Harry's grasp of the game. He handled his paper money confidently, and bought and sold properties with unexpected acumen. It looked as if, like it or not, he had some of his father's blood in him!

She was losing quite heavily when a man's shadow fell over the board.

'Hello, Rafe,' Kate said absently, without looking round. 'You're back early.' Then she nodded to Harry. 'Come on, it's your go.'

But Harry's small face had gone quite pale, and he was staring up with a slightly frantic expression in his eyes. Kate felt a rash of goose-pimples race over her skin, and she slowly turned her head.

It wasn't Rafe who was standing behind her. It was a much bigger and more muscular man. Kate recognised him at once—after all, she was the one who had nicknamed him 'Gorilla'. It was the man who had been Harry's bodyguard at Martin Foster's villa.

A great rush of despair swept over her as she stared up at him. All they had been through—and now it looked as if it had all been for nothing. They were just a couple of days away from reuniting Harry with his mother, and suddenly it had gone disastrously wrong. For one wild moment, she thought of trying to bribe the bodyguard. She'd offer him money—*anything*. But she took another look at his face, and knew it would never work. They had got the better of him once, and made him look a complete fool. He hadn't forgotten that, and now he was about to get his own back.

'How—how did you find us?' she asked shakily.

'We've had men watching the coast road,' he growled at her, with some satisfaction. 'Just on the off chance that you were still in the area. Your car was spotted yesterday. It wasn't too hard to follow you back here, and find where you were holed up.'

Kate briefly closed her eyes. That one innocent day out—and it had led to their discovery. And it was all her fault. *She* was the one who had suggested the day at the beach.

'What are you going to do?' she said, with mounting apprehension.

'I'm taking Harry back to his father.'

Harry jumped to his feet. *'No!'* he roared. 'I don't want to go!'

The bodyguard ignored him, and instead looked at Kate. 'You'd better persuade the boy that he *does* want to go,' he warned meaningfully.

Kate quickly got the message. She suppressed a huge shiver, and turned to Harry. 'We'd better just go and find out what your father wants. It'll be all right,' she said, blinking back her own tears at the boy's distress. 'I'll come with you.' She turned back to the bodyguard. 'I can come, can't I?'

'Oh, yes, you can come,' he confirmed. 'Mr Foster is *very* anxious to see you.'

This time, Kate couldn't stop the shiver that ran right through her. Surreptitiously, she glanced at her watch. Where was Rafe? He was always right behind her when she didn't want him to be. Yet now that she really needed him, he wasn't here.

Part of her knew that she was being unreasonable, that Rafe couldn't possibly have known that this would happen. She couldn't help it, though. She was so scared, and so sick at the thought of having to return Harry to his father.

'I'll need to get some things,' she said, trying to play for time.

'All you need to bring is the boy,' replied the bodyguard roughly. 'Let's get moving.'

For one wild moment, Kate contemplated grabbing Harry and making a run for it. Then, with a resigned sigh, she abandoned that idea. They wouldn't get more than a few yards before the gorilla caught up with them. Anyway, it might end up in a scuffle, with Harry caught up in the middle of it. She couldn't risk letting him get hurt in any way.

'Come on, Harry,' she said gently, holding out her hand to him. Her heart turned over as he looked up at her with fearful, miserable eyes. In just minutes, the laughing, happy Harry of the last few days had disappeared, and he had become the tense, unhappy child she had first seen at Martin Foster's villa.

'Do we have to?' he asked in a small voice.

'I'm afraid so. But don't worry,' she said, with far more confidence than she felt. 'Everything will turn out all right.'

They followed the bodyguard out to his car. Kate still kept looking around, hoping—praying—that Rafe would miraculously appear and rescue them. It didn't happen, though. She and Harry were bundled into the back seat, and the car drove quickly away from the Villa des Anges.

She held Harry's hand very tightly all through the short drive. When they reached Martin Foster's sumptuous villa, though, the bodyguard rather roughly separated them.

'You're to go to your room, Harry,' he instructed. 'The housekeeper will bring you your lunch.'

Harry shot a pleading look at Kate.

'Let me go with him,' Kate begged the guard, a little desperately. 'He needs me.'

'No, he doesn't,' replied the guard implacably. 'This is his home. He'll be fine on his own.' He turned to Harry. 'Up to your room,' he instructed again. Harry aimed a last desperate look at Kate; then he turned round and trudged slowly up the stairs, a picture of utter dejection. Kate could hardly bear to watch. How could anyone do this to a small child?

'You're to come with me,' ordered the bodyguard when Harry was finally out of sight.

'To see Mr Foster?' she asked, hearing a humiliating quaver in her own voice.

'Mr Foster won't be back until tomorrow,' the guard informed her. 'He's gone to St Tropez. He remembered the two of you told him you were heading that way, and he's gone to try and find you. He knew it was a long shot, but it was the only lead he had.'

'You're going to keep me here until he gets back?' Kate asked with growing trepidation.

'Yes,' confirmed the bodyguard, with some relish. 'Mr Foster's going to be pleased to see his boy back.' Then he grinned malevolently. 'But I don't know quite how he's going to feel when he sees you.' He gave Kate a painful prod in the side. 'Get moving, up those stairs.'

A couple of minutes later, Kate found herself locked in a bedroom at the rear of the villa. There was a small bathroom leading off it, and she ran the cold-water tap, then splashed some on to her face. She had suddenly begun to feel rather light-headed, and needed something to revive her.

Feeling just a little better, she walked back into the bedroom and sat on the edge of the bed. Was that gorilla really going to keep her locked in here until Martin Foster returned? It looked like it. And what would happen then? she wondered with a shudder.

She concentrated her thoughts instead on Harry, back in this house that he hated, despite all the promises she and Rafe had made to him that he would be reunited with his mother. She felt as if she had let him down so very badly, and would have given anything to be able to put things right for him again.

After a while, she stopped thinking altogether, and just sat there with her hands clasped tightly together to stop them shaking. And she was still sitting like that nearly two hours later, when the door finally opened again.

For a moment, blind hope rushed through her. Were they going to let her out? Perhaps they had decided to let her stay with Harry after all. Then she saw Rafe walk slowly through the door. The gorilla was standing just behind him. As soon as Rafe was inside the room, the bodyguard gave a triumphant grin, closed the door, and locked it again.

Kate didn't even think what she was doing. She just flew across the room, straight into Rafe's arms.

He held her very tight for a few moments. Then he pushed her away from him and took a good look at her. 'Are you all right?' he asked roughly. 'That ape didn't hurt you?'

She shook her head. 'No. Nor Harry. But they wouldn't let me stay with him,' she said in some distress.

'Harry will be fine,' he calmed her. 'He might not like being here, but he'll be in good hands. These people all work for Martin Foster—they're going to make sure they take very good care of his son.'

'But he was so miserable!'

'I know. But we can't do anything about that right now,' Rafe said in a frustrated tone.

Kate raised her head, ready to say something else. Then she saw his face clearly for the first time, and she caught her breath. There were cuts and bruises around his eyes and jaw, and she saw him wince slightly as he moved.

'Who did that?' she demanded. 'The gorilla?'

Rafe smiled ruefully. 'He finally got his revenge.'

'Why didn't you fight back? Why didn't you put the famous armlock on him, the way you did last time?'

'What a bloodthirsty child you are!' he commented. 'But you're right, I don't usually stand around and let someone beat me to a pulp. This time, the advantages were rather on his side, though.'

Kate fished a handkerchief out of her pocket, and dabbed rather ineffectually at his face. 'What do you mean?'

'He made it clear that if I laid a finger on him he'd take it out on you,' Rafe told her reluctantly.

She stared at him. 'What?'

He gave a brief shrug. 'How do you suppose he got me here without a struggle? I don't usually let someone lock me into a room without putting up a fight. He described rather graphically what he'd do to you, though, if I gave him the slightest trouble.'

'Oh,' said Kate, in a small voice. 'You mean——?'

'I mean that if I want you to stay healthy and unhurt, I've got to go along with whatever that gorilla wants. If I don't, then you're the one who'll suffer.'

'He's probably bluffing,' said Kate, with a rather poor attempt at bravado.

'Perhaps he is. But I'm not going to risk it,' Rafe said with complete finality.

'And you let him beat you up, rather than see me get hurt?' She gave an audible gulp. 'No one's ever done anything like that for me before.'

'I didn't do it willingly,' he admitted drily. 'There just didn't seem to be much of an alternative.' Then he gave her a faintly impatient shake. 'Kate, will you stop looking at me with hero-worship written all over your face?'

'I can't help it,' she said simply.

He gave a small growl under his breath, but didn't seem exactly displeased.

A couple of minutes later, he made his way to the bathroom and came back with a cold flannel held to the worst of the bruises on his face.

'Do you know how long we're going to be kept locked in here?' he asked her.

'Until tomorrow, I think,' she replied worriedly. 'That's when Martin Foster's coming back. He's in St Tropez at the moment, looking for us.' Then she glanced at Rafe rather anxiously. 'What do you suppose he'll do then? Will he hand us over to the police?'

'I shouldn't think so,' replied Rafe. 'Legally, he's on very shaky ground. We shouldn't have taken Harry, but neither should he. And he's certainly got no right to keep us locked up like this. I very much doubt if he'll want to get involved with the law.'

'Then—what *will* he do?' she asked hesitantly.

'I think he'll want to deal with us himself,' Rafe told her reluctantly, after a short pause.

Kate decided that she didn't like the sound of that, and rather nervously twisted her fingers together. 'Isn't there something we can do?'

'Not much. Only sit and wait for Martin Foster to return.'

'You're being very calm about this!'

Rafe's gaze fixed on her. 'What do you want me to do? Panic? Hammer on the door and demand to be let out? Make wild plans for getting out of here? None of that would do us any good, Kate,' he told her levelly.

She already knew that. All the same, it didn't mean she had to like it!

'I thought you'd be really good in this sort of situation,' she said edgily. 'You're turning out to be something of a disappointment.'

'Not Superman, after all?' There was a note of dry amusement in his voice. 'Sorry, Kate.'

But her flash of frustrated annoyance had already passed. And she really didn't mind that he wasn't Superman. It made him seem—well, much more human and approachable, she decided. Not the half devil that her mother had so often accused him of being, but just someone who coped with different situations in the way he thought best. No flashy heroics, no pointless gestures of macho bravery—only calm decisions, based on sound judgement. Kate realised that she actually much preferred that. It made her feel a lot safer.

The afternoon seemed to drag by with dreadful slowness. Neither of them spoke very much, but the silence that stretched between them wasn't uncomfortable.

Around five o'clock, the lock on the door suddenly clicked open. Kate jumped visibly, but Rafe remained very still. A moment later, the door opened and the bodyguard appeared in the doorway, carrying a tray. He put it down on the floor, and then grinned unpleasantly at them.

'Make the most of it,' he advised. 'It's the only meal you're going to get.' Then he closed and locked the door again, and something inside Kate seemed to become unbearably tense as she heard the lock click back into place.

Rafe picked up the tray and put it on the small table by the window. 'Want something to eat?' he asked.

But Kate couldn't even bear to look at the food. 'I—I want to wash my hands first,' she mumbled. Then she hurriedly went into the bathroom, and shut the door.

Once inside, she took a couple of deep breaths and tried to fight back the sudden attack of panic that had swept over her. 'If Rafe can cope with this, then so can you,' she argued with herself through clenched teeth. Gradually, her breathing eased a little and her legs stopped shaking. She ran her fingers through her hair, fixed a smile on to her face, and then went back into the bedroom.

'I think I'll have something to eat now,' she said to Rafe, just a little too casually.

Rafe saw through her pretence straight away. 'You don't have to behave like this—not with me,' he told her bluntly. 'If you're scared stiff, then just say so. If you want to kick at something because you're sick of being cooped up in here, then just do it.'

'Thank you, but I'm fine,' Kate said in a brittle voice.

'You don't look—or sound—fine to me.' He came over and closed his hands around her own. 'It'll be all right, Kate,' he said, holding her gaze levelly. 'I promise you that.'

She somehow managed a shaky smile. 'I do like a man who's sure of himself.'

His eyes briefly glittered. 'Do you?' he said softly. Then he slowly let go of her hands again, as if he were very reluctant to release her. 'Come and have something to eat. It'll make you feel better.'

Kate sat down opposite him and found that, miraculously, her appetite had returned. She managed to eat everything on her plate, and then sat back with a small sigh.

'You're right, I *do* feel better.' Then her brows drew together in a worried frown. 'I hope Harry's OK.'

'Harry's pretty resilient,' Rafe reassured her. 'He'll come through this all right. Kids are good at surviving the kind of emotional traumas that would knock most adults right off their feet.'

Kate just hoped he was right. She couldn't help remembering Harry's unhappy little face, though, as he had reluctantly gone up those stairs to his room.

Dusk closed in outside, and then passed with its usual swiftness. There was a velvet darkness outside the windows, and a huge moon shimmered on the horizon, spreading its pale silvery light over the sea. Scented air drifted in through the window, which was still open because of the warmth of the night, and lights from other villas twinkled softly in the distance. Kate sat and looked at the scene, but it seemed faintly unreal. Perhaps it was because she was suddenly very tired, she told herself, stifling a huge yawn.

'Sleepy?' asked Rafe. 'Why don't you turn in for the night?' Then, seeing the faintly troubled look on her face, he gave her a gently mocking smile. 'You can have the bed. I'll take the chair.'

'You won't be very comfortable,' she warned.

'No, I won't,' he agreed, his eyes briefly glittering. 'But it doesn't matter. I don't feel much like sleeping.'

Kate trailed into the bathroom, had a quick wash, and then wrinkled her nose as she tried to rub her teeth clean with a corner of the flannel. Then she stared at her reflection in the mirror.

She was slightly disturbed to find that she didn't look quite herself. Her eyes seemed much bigger than usual, there was a faint flush to her skin, and her mouth was set into a troubled line.

'Just try to relax and get a good night's sleep,' she advised herself. 'You're going to need it if you're going to get through tomorrow!'

She returned to the bedroom and switched off the light. Then, still fully dressed, she stretched out on the bed, keeping her back to Rafe, who was sitting quietly in the chair by the window. With some determination, she closed her eyes; then, against all expectations, she fell asleep.

When she opened her eyes again, the room was still dark. She had no idea what time it was, but when she turned her head towards the window she could see that the moon was much higher in the sky, and she guessed that a couple of hours had passed. Rafe was still sitting in exactly the same position, though. He didn't look as if he had moved a single inch.

Kate felt a little odd—sort of half asleep and rather disorientated. She sat up, and Rafe immediately turned to look at her.

'I think you'd better stay where you are, Kate,' he said softly.

But Kate was already on her feet, and walking towards him. Rafe shifted slightly restlessly, and Kate had the impression that he was unexpectedly tense. She didn't really care, though. She felt very much on her own right now, and she didn't like it. She needed human company.

As she reached his side, the moonlight fell full on to Rafe's face, illuminating it quite clearly. Not that it made very much difference, though, because his expression was quite unreadable. Kate gave a silent sigh. Why was Rafe being so unapproachable just when she needed him?

Needed him? she repeated to herself, in faint surprise. Then she slowly relaxed again. Somehow, the idea didn't seem in the least strange. Perhaps it was just the darkness, the huge moon, the velvet silence of the night—or perhaps it was something else. Kate didn't know, and she found that she didn't particularly care.

Rafe stood up. 'I think you should have stayed where you were,' he told her, and she gave a faint inner shiver as she heard the husky tone of his voice.

'I didn't want to,' she answered quietly.

Rafe let out a slightly unsteady breath. 'It's very late. And I'm not in the mood for talking.'

'I don't want to talk,' Kate said simply. 'I just want company.'

'And I want——' His voice broke off, and he gave a dry smile. 'You know perfectly well what I want. That's why it's not a very good idea for you to come too close.'

Kate didn't move, though.

'You're still too near,' he warned her.

'I know.' But her feet stayed exactly where they were. 'I wish I could work out how I feel about you,' Kate went on, in a low tone. 'A lot of the time you really confuse me. Did you know that?'

'Is that why you keep running away from me?'

'I suppose so,' she admitted. 'It was safer than . . .'

'Than what, Kate?' he prompted gently.

But she decided that she had already said far more than she had ever meant to. 'I don't know,' she muttered. 'I'm probably just talking nonsense.'

'Then keep on doing it,' Rafe encouraged. 'I like listening to that sort of nonsense.'

He moved, and his shadow blocked out the moon. Without that pale light, she couldn't see his face, couldn't tell what he was thinking—or intended doing.

'Rafe——' she began uncertainly.

'And I like it when you say my name,' he interrupted her. 'Especially when you say it in that particular way.'

Kate knew that it was definitely time to back off, but her feet still wouldn't move. Rafe shifted position, and the moonlight was back on his face again now, clearly illuminating his features. Kate softly caught her breath. His eyes glinted brightly in the silvery light, and it was all too easy to read the message written in them. It was very late at night, they were in dangerous circumstances, which always heightened the senses, and she had pushed him just a little too far. Unless she put an end to this right now, she was going to end up in serious trouble.

And yet, *still* she didn't move.

Kate couldn't understand it. Here she was, with Rafe advancing on her with increasingly single-minded intent, and she wasn't doing a single thing to stop him. With a fierce sense of shock, she realised that she didn't actually *want* to stop him.

Which was crazy, of course. When he bent his head and kissed her—which he was going to do any moment now—she would realise just how crazy it was. Then she would be sorry that she hadn't backed out while she'd still had the chance.

His kiss came just an instant later—and she wasn't sorry at all. She revelled in the hard, warm touch of his mouth, and wanted it to go on forever.

It didn't, though. Rafe was already moving on to other things. His hands shifted over her with a sureness which she loved, and her skin seemed to melt at the intimate contact.

He moved up closer, leaning slightly against her now, so that she could feel the full, aroused length of him. 'We really do seem very—compatible, Kate,' he murmured in her ear.

Although she hadn't meant to, Kate found herself smiling. Rafe saw the smile, and seemed pleased. Then he began to ease away her clothes. Kate meant to make one last feeble protest, but somehow it never came out. And then it was too late because Rafe's mouth had closed over hers again, cutting off all hope of being able to say a single word.

She was nervous and yet, at the same time, felt extraordinarily safe. She told herself that that was mad, because she was certain that no female could ever be completely safe around Rafe Clarendon. But he was so sure of himself that he gave her confidence, and he was gentle enough to ease all of her deeply buried fears.

His breathing was heavier now, and she knew that he was having to work hard to control it. His shirt was open and she thought that she must have undone it, although she couldn't remember actually touching the buttons. She could smell the warm, musky scent of him, and she liked it; she bent her head and rubbed her cheek against his chest, like a healthy young animal greeting its mate.

Rafe's fingers instantly responded, tracing their way down the line of her spine and then locking together, imprisoning her against him. Kate caught her breath. She was beginning to ache as much as he did. She hadn't expected it to happen like this, so quickly, so urgently, so very fiercely.

He paused for an instant, and caught his breath. 'If you still want to run away, you'd better do it right now,' he warned a little roughly.

'I don't want to run,' she said softly.

'Just remember that I gave you the chance,' Rafe murmured huskily. Then he didn't say any more. Instead, he picked her up, and in just seconds she felt the coolness of the sheets against her back. Her *bare* back. When had she lost the last of her clothes? She couldn't remember, and that disturbed her. But she was disturbed even more by the light licking of Rafe's tongue as he explored at random, finding all her most sensitive pulse-points and making them flare into life.

'Mmm,' he murmured appreciatively. 'You taste much nicer without all that salt on your skin.'

'I don't—don't think you should be doing that,' Kate got out feebly as he continued to take the most outrageous liberties with her compliant body.

'Why not?' He raised his head and grinned wickedly at her. 'Want to do it to *me*?' he invited softly.

'No!' Kate was shocked to her very soul. And then she was even more shocked by the realisation that she hadn't actually meant 'no' at all.

His hands flickered over her breasts, skimming the soft underswell, dancing over the achingly hard tips, and teasing to the point of torment.

She gave a faint groan of frustration, and he seemed pleased by that. The teasing stopped immediately, though, to be replaced by the firm clasp of his palm, just holding her.

Kate looked up at him, and in the darkness she could just make out the shape of his face, and the dark glitter of his eyes. He seemed incredibly familiar, as if she had known him all her life.

Well, you *have* known him on and off for years, she reminded herself. But this was a very different kind of knowing—and yet it felt completely right, perfectly normal. As if they had always been meant to end up like this.

Rafe eased up against her, and she wasn't in the least nervous of the evidence of his quite fierce arousal.

'Not scared, Kate?' he challenged softly, almost as if he could read her thoughts.

She gave a brief shake of her head.

'I won't hurt you,' he assured her.

'I know you won't,' she said, amazed at her own confidence.

Then a look of unexpected uncertainty came over his face. 'Perhaps I should never have started this,' he muttered. His face cleared again in an instant, though. 'Too late now,' he said with renewed fierceness. 'Much too late...'

Kate already knew that. And she didn't care. This was *Rafe*, and somehow that made it all right. She didn't know how or why—it was just a fact of life, like the sun coming up in the morning, or the birds singing at dawn.

As he moved his weight over her, she slid her arms around him easily and naturally. His skin was hot and smooth against her fingertips. It felt good, and she told him so, although not with words.

He eased closer, and her body was all vivid sensation now. She knew that it was the same for him— she could feel his muscles tense, his nerve-ends leap, his skin begin to burn.

Her hands moved of their own accord; it was incredible, almost magic. They touched him, held him, imprisoned and released again. Rafe groaned out loud, and she liked that. She wanted to make him do it again. But he was past the stage where he could endure

more teasing. With a fierce growl, he caught hold of
her wrists. Then he shifted over her and into her in
one fluid movement.

The ease of it astonished her. No pain, no awk-
wardness; only a purely natural joining of two bodies
that seemed to fit together with astounding per-
fection. Then Rafe began to move again, and Kate
was caught up in an entirely new whirl of surprise.
She was enchanted by the care he took, dazzled by
the extraordinary sensations that swept over her, and
then she trembled as the rhythm gathered speed,
spinning her on to another plane.

But Rafe was shaking, too, and somehow that made
it all right. Whatever was happening between them
was shared, and if she was helpless, then so was he.
And he *was* out of control now, but it didn't matter,
it wasn't important, because the final shudder that
ran through him echoed right through her as well,
and it was glorious to share so much pleasure. Glorious, and mystifying, and just a little frightening. But
as Kate slowly floated back to reality, she knew that
she didn't want to change one single second of it. And
she wouldn't have wanted this to have happened with
anyone except Rafe.

His full weight slumped against her for a while
longer. Then he raised his head and looked down at
her.

'All right?' he murmured in a tired but totally relaxed voice.

Kate simply nodded her head. She couldn't possibly have found enough words to tell him just how all
right everything was. She didn't care that they were
still locked in this room. She didn't even care about

what tomorrow might bring. At this precise moment, everything was incredibly perfect.

And that included Rafe, she told herself as she curled against him and closed her eyes. Then she smiled at the thought of Rafe Clarendon being perfect.

Rafe—just the sound of his name pleased her. She was still thinking about how much she liked, loved, adored this man, when she fell asleep.

CHAPTER NINE

KATE woke up in the morning with an extraordinary sense of well-being that didn't seem to make any sense to her for a while. Then the events of last night began to trickle back into her mind, and she almost stopped breathing.

She kept her eyes very tightly closed while she thought about it. With luck, Rafe would think she was still asleep. She didn't want any eye-to-eye contact with him until she had got used to the idea of what had happened between them.

'Going to fake sleep all morning, Kate?' enquired a familiar voice.

Very reluctantly, Kate opened her eyes. Rafe was sitting on the edge of the bed, fully dressed, and looking down at her with some interest. Automatically, she grabbed the sheet and hauled it right up to her chin.

'It's a little late for that,' he reminded her with a huge grin. 'Anyway, you're not the modest type.'

'You don't know that——' she began defensively. Then her face went a glowing scarlet. He certainly *did* know it.

Oh, Kate, what have you done? she asked herself slightly desperately. And with *Rafe*, out of all the men you could have chosen.

But you didn't want any of the others, a small voice inside her head reminded her. You wanted Rafe Clarendon. And it's too late now to change your mind.

When love hits you, it's never just a gentle tap on the shoulder. It always wallops you right off your feet.

Her eyebrows shot up. Love? When had love come into it? Some time during the night? Or had it been hovering in the background for a long time now, just waiting for a chance to catch her off guard?

Kate groaned out loud, suddenly feeling absolutely weighed down with the enormity of what had happened.

Rafe's eyes narrowed. 'Regretting it already?' he asked, his tone a shade cooler.

'No,' she admitted. 'It's just that—well, it's come as a bit of a shock.'

His features relaxed again. 'If the circumstances were different, I'd like to give you a few more shocks,' he murmured. Then his voice became brisker. 'But right now, you'd better get into some clothes. That bodyguard could come barging in at any moment, and I don't want him to see you like that.'

Kate had almost forgotten that they were locked in the bedroom of Martin Foster's villa. Rafe's words made her grab her clothes, though, and scuttle into the bathroom.

She had a quick wash, and hurriedly dressed. Then she glanced at herself in the mirror. She didn't look all that different. She certainly *felt* different, though. And all because of Rafe...

She went back into the bedroom feeling oddly shy. Rafe looked up and smiled at her as she came in, and almost immediately she began to feel better. Then she took a closer look at him, and saw that the marks on his face were already beginning to turn a rather angry purple.

'I forgot about your bruises last night,' she said rather anxiously. 'I didn't hurt you, did I?'

'I don't know,' he said simply. 'I don't remember.'

Kate looked at him severely. 'Are you telling me you've forgotten the whole thing already?'

'No. Just that I only remember the good parts.' He got up and moved closer. 'And they were *very* good, Kate,' he said softly.

Her heart thumped, and her knees gently began to knock. Rafe took another step towards her, and her head was just beginning to go dizzy with anticipation when they both heard the door being unlocked. Rafe quickly moved back again, and there was a couple of feet of space between them by the time the bodyguard opened the door and walked into the room.

He studied Rafe's marked face with some satisfaction. 'Not so good-looking as you were yesterday, are you?' he taunted him.

Rafe didn't rise to the bait. 'You do know that it's illegal to hold us like this?' he enquired evenly.

The bodyguard seemed unconcerned. 'Mr Foster returned early this morning,' he informed them. 'He's waiting to see you.'

Kate felt her skin grow cold. As she and Rafe moved towards the door, Rafe briefly laid his hand on her shoulder. 'Everything will be fine,' he said in a low undertone.

The sound of his voice gave her courage. 'Of course it will be,' she said, with a fairly successful attempt at a smile. Then they followed the bodyguard down the stairs, and into a large drawing-room at the front of the villa.

Martin Foster was standing by the window. As they came in he turned to face them, and Kate could see his eyes were ice-cold.

With one brief gesture, he dismissed the bodyguard. Then he stared at the two of them with pure contempt.

'I knew it had to be you who had taken away my son,' he said in clipped tones. 'What sort of people are you, who can take a child away from his father?'

Kate could hardly believe that she was hearing this. 'But that's exactly what *you* did,' she said indignantly, taking a step forward. 'You snatched Harry away from his mother! That was a *terrible* thing to do.'

Martin Foster looked rather taken aback, as if he hadn't expected to be challenged in this way. He quickly recovered himself, though.

'That's absolutely no excuse for your own outrageous behaviour. It was illegal and immoral.'

'I believe it was also illegal for you to take Harry in the first place,' Rafe pointed out evenly. 'Especially as the court had awarded custody to his mother.'

'He's my son!' Martin Foster said belligerently. 'I've every right to have him here with me.'

'You're making him sound like a possession,' Kate said angrily. 'We're talking about a child! All right, so he's your son, but that doesn't give you the right to turn his life upside-down, and make him thoroughly miserable. Anyway, surely the most important thing is to have a child who loves you?'

Martin Foster's gaze swivelled round to fix on her. 'Are you telling me that my son doesn't love me?' he said in a soft and yet extremely menacing voice.

'Kate,' warned Rafe, with a light touch on her arm.

But Kate couldn't think of anything except Harry right now. 'No, he doesn't love you,' she said boldly. 'He doesn't even know you! You dragged him away from his mother and brought him here, but have you spent any time with him? Have you talked to him, bothered to find out how he feels, what *he* wants?'

'He's six years old,' Martin Foster replied tautly. 'When he's old enough to have opinions of his own, then I'll discuss things with him. A boy of six needs discipline, firm guidance and a good education.'

'He also needs love and attention,' retorted Kate stubbornly. 'And the freedom to develop his own interests and ideas. Believe it or not, Harry already has fairly strong opinions on a lot of things—including his own future. He wants to be with his mother,' she finished bluntly.

'You're not getting through to him, Kate,' Rafe said quietly. 'Men like Martin Foster only ever see things from their own point of view.'

But it was desperately important to Kate that she *did* get through. Harry's whole future might depend on it.

She turned back to Martin Foster. 'Don't you care that your son doesn't love you?' she said a little despairingly. 'That he's actually scared of you?'

A flicker of response finally showed in Martin Foster's eyes. 'Nonsense!' he said sharply. 'My son couldn't possibly be scared of me. I've given him everything——'

'You've snatched him away from his mother, and from his home,' Kate interrupted fiercely. 'You've shoved him into a strange house where he knows no one, and my guess is that you've virtually ignored him.

Just having him here was enough for you, wasn't it? You didn't think you had to do any more. But you've got to give up a huge chunk of your time if you want to be a real father.'

'I'm a very busy man,' came his short response. There wasn't quite so much certainty in his voice this time, though, and Kate drew in a deep breath.

'You've still got to make time for the things that are important in your life. If you don't, you'll end up not only with a failed marriage, but with a son who's going to grow up resenting and disliking you. Is that what you want?' she challenged him directly.

For just a moment, Martin Foster looked uncertain again. Then the hardness spread back over his face, and his eyes shone coldly. 'I won't have two strangers coming here and telling me how to run my life,' he said tautly. 'Do you hear me? *I won't have it!*'

But Kate wouldn't be browbeaten. 'Well, some-one's got to tell you. And someone's got to try and stop you ruining Harry's life. Why won't you understand? Your son is thoroughly miserable and un-happy. If you don't believe me, ask him for yourself!'

Martin Foster stared at her with fierce anger. Then he walked over and opened the door. The bodyguard was standing just outside. 'Bring Harry down here,' Martin Foster instructed him. Then he walked slowly back into the drawing-room. 'I accept that Harry has had some difficulties in adapting to the sudden change of circumstances,' he said in a terse voice. 'But I do *not* accept any of your other accusations. And once you hear the truth from Harry yourself, perhaps you'll realise just how much damage you've done during these last few days.'

He said nothing more until the door opened. Harry stood there uncertainly for a moment. Then he saw Rafe and Kate, and his face lit up.

'Have you come to take me home?' he asked excitedly.

'Harry!' Martin Foster walked over to stand in front of his son. '*This* is your home now,' he told him sternly.

Harry's face fell. 'It's not my *real* home,' he mumbled.

'This is a beautiful house,' Martin Foster responded in a sharp tone. 'You should be grateful to live here.'

Harry's mouth drooped at the corners. 'I don't like it here.'

Kate went over and crouched down beside him. 'Why don't you like it?' she asked quietly.

'There's no one to play with. I haven't got any friends. And I can't go to school. I don't go out, and we have boiled eggs for breakfast every morning, and *never* any custard. No one talks to me. I miss my dog, his name's Sam, and me and my mummy take him for walks. I want to go home, I don't want to stay here.' Harry finally ran out of breath. Then he looked up at Kate. 'Why doesn't my mummy come and get me?' he asked, his lip quivering.

Kate blinked her own eyes rather hard. 'You'd better ask your father that question,' she said quietly.

But Harry wouldn't even look at his father. Instead, he went over to Rafe and clung tightly on to his hand.

Kate turned back to Martin Foster, and found that he was looking extremely shaken by Harry's outburst.

'Are you going to answer Harry's question?' she asked quietly.

'I didn't know the boy felt like that,' he muttered. Then his features became fierce again. 'Someone should have told me!'

Rafe took a step forward, still holding firmly on to Harry. 'It isn't up to your staff to find out these things. Harry is *your* son. You're the one who should know what's going on in his life.'

Martin Foster paced up and down a couple of times. Then he turned and shot a dark look at Rafe. 'I still think the boy should stay with me. I'm his father. I've a right to have him.'

Kate shook her head. 'Instead of talking about rights, why don't you try and work out where Harry would be happiest? Surely that's the only important thing?'

'But according to you that's with his mother,' Martin Foster retorted.

'That's right,' agreed Rafe. 'But Jillie's a very reasonable person. I'm sure she'd be willing to let you see Harry whenever you wanted. She won't try and keep Harry away from you, just to be spiteful and vindictive.'

Martin Foster was only half listening, though. He was also looking at Harry, who was steadfastly refusing to look back at him. He couldn't seem to believe that he couldn't bend this small boy to his will, the way he did with so many of the adults who worked for him.

'Is that really what you want, Harry?' he said at last, with heavy reluctance. 'To go back to your mother, and stay with her?'

Harry immediately brightened up. 'Yes,' he said in a very definite voice.

At that, his father's face changed quite dramatically. It was as if he was finally facing up to something that he had quite deliberately ignored for a very long time.

A tense silence descended on the room, until Kate couldn't stand it any more. 'What are you going to do?' she asked in a low voice. 'Are you going to let us take him home?'

Martin Foster half turned away from them. 'Do I have any choice?' he said at last, obviously finding it an enormous effort to force the words out.

Harry looked up at Kate uncertainly. 'Am I going back to my mummy?' he asked in a loud whisper.

Kate gave him a big grin. 'Yes, I think you are.'

Harry let out an exuberant whoop of joy, and Martin Foster turned back to stare at him, as if he was really looking at his son properly for the first time.

'Aren't you going to thank me, Harry?'

Harry lowered his eyes. 'Thank you,' he mumbled, scuffling his feet uncomfortably.

Martin Foster looked at Rafe with an uncharacteristic uncertainty in his eyes. 'Will it ever get any better between us?' he muttered, his features dark.

'Yes, of course,' Rafe replied firmly. 'But you're going to have to give it time, and you're going to have to work at it.'

Harry's father slowly nodded. 'I suppose you're right. Now, you'd better get him out of here,' he added slightly harshly, 'before I change my mind.'

Rafe held on to Harry's hand, slid an arm around Kate's shoulder, and shepherded the two of them out of the room.

*   *   *

In a couple of days, Jillie came to collect Harry and take him back home. She looked pale, but absolutely overjoyed to be reunited with her son.

Jillie was every bit as beautiful as Kate had thought she would be, and she felt a strong pang of pure jealousy when she first saw Jillie and Rafe together. Then she slowly started to relax again as it became clear that there was nothing between them except an easy friendship. In fact, once Jillie had finished profusely thanking the two of them for getting Harry back for her, she only had eyes for her son.

Jillie and Harry stayed at the villa overnight. In the morning, Rafe would drive them to the airport, so they could catch an early flight back to England.

Kate found it a real wrench when it was finally time to say goodbye to Harry. She had grown very fond of him, and was looking forward to taking up Jillie's invitation to come and visit them as soon as she got the chance.

She stood at the door, waving, until the car was finally out of sight. Then she trailed slowly back into the villa.

It seemed very quiet and empty. Kate wandered around, feeling slightly on edge. These were the first moments she had had to herself for ages, but she wasn't sure that she was enjoying it very much. It gave her too much opportunity to think about everything that had happened—and about Rafe.

Just the sound of his name, when she said it out loud, made her nerves jump. So much had altered between them, and yet she still didn't really know where she stood. They had been so caught up in Harry's problems that there hadn't been much time to talk about their own.

She was almost glad when she heard the phone ring. She was beginning to find the silence rather oppressive. When she picked up the receiver, though, she gave a small grimace when she heard her mother's voice at the other end.

She had phoned her father last night, and given him a potted—and very expurgated!—version of what had happened. He had taken it all quite calmly, and Kate had been glad of that, but she had known that news of what had been going on would eventually trickle down to her mother. And she definitely *couldn't* be relied on to take it so calmly.

'Kate, I can't believe what your father's been telling me,' announced her mother, launching straight into the attack. 'You should have come straight home as soon as you found out that man was staying at Great-Uncle Henry's villa. Some men are born to cause trouble, and Rafe Clarendon is one of them!'

'You really don't know him well enough to make a sweeping judgement like that,' Kate protested.

'I've *heard* about him. And some of the stories would make your hair curl,' said her mother darkly.

'My hair already curls,' retorted Kate. 'And I don't think people should listen to that kind of gossip. Most of it's either made up or highly exaggerated.'

'Are you defending that man? After all the trouble he got you into?'

'I was the one who insisted on staying. He tried really hard to get rid of me, but I wouldn't go. None of what happened was his fault, and, anyway, it all turned out very well in the end.'

'There you go, defending him again!' said her mother in exasperation. 'What is it about men like that? They always find women willing to make excuses for their behaviour.' Then her voice suddenly took on a suspicious note. 'Or is there something you haven't told me, Kate?' she demanded. 'What has that man been up to?'

'Nothing,' Kate answered, just a little too quickly. 'At least, nothing that I haven't wanted him to get up to,' she amended wryly. 'And why do you keep calling him "that man"? He does have a name!' Before her mother could get in another word, she added, 'I've got to go now. I'll ring you later,' and she very firmly put down the receiver.

Ruffled by the conversation, Kate stalked out on to the terrace and flopped on to a sun-lounger. She knew that she would have to ring her mother later and apologise, but she wasn't looking forward to it. Sooner or later, her mother would bring the conversation back to the subject of Rafe Clarendon, and Kate didn't want to talk about him just now. Things were still too unsettled between them, and she had no idea how all of this was eventually going to turn out.

As if the mention of his name had magically conjured him up, Rafe appeared on the terrace. Kate swallowed hard as she saw him, and sat up as he walked towards her.

'Did they catch their plane all right?' she asked as he seated himself beside her.

'No problem,' he assured her. 'Why didn't you come to the airport with us?'

'I hate saying goodbye,' she admitted. 'I'd have probably started blubbering, and then we'd have all ended up in tears.'

'Well, Harry sent his love, and he's looking forward to you going to visit them.'

'Do you really think they'll be able to sort things out?' she asked a little anxiously. 'Martin Foster won't suddenly have a change of heart, and try to grab Harry back again?'

Rafe shook his head. 'I don't think so. He got a severe shock that day, hearing his own son telling him he didn't want to stay with him. That kind of thing stays with you for a very long time, and can really change your life. And talking of changes,' he went on, his tone altering quite noticeably, 'I thought I'd better tell you that I'm going back to England myself in a couple of days.'

'Going——' Kate gulped, and made another stab at it. 'Going back?'

'This was never a holiday for me,' he reminded her. 'Only a job of work. And I've got more work lined up for the rest of the summer. Much as I'd like to, I can't stay here sunning myself for the next few weeks.'

'Oh,' she said, rather inadequately.

'What about your own plans?' he asked casually. 'You told me you wanted to try and write a novel. Is that still on the cards?'

'I'm definitely going to have a go.'

'The villa would be an ideal place for writing,' Rafe pointed out. 'It's very tranquil and quiet.'

'It is when you're not around,' Kate said drily. Then she looked at him uncertainly. 'Are you telling me that you want me to stay here, while you go back to England?'

His dark gaze rested on her. 'No, I'm not saying that at all. I'm just giving you the chance to run away from me again—if you still want to.'

'Oh,' she said again, slightly flummoxed. 'Then—er—what's the alternative?'

'You could come back to England with me,' he said comfortably.

'Back to England——?' She blinked at him, and tried to work out exactly what he was saying. 'You mean, I'd live with my parents and we'd sort of carry on getting to know each other?' she said slowly.

'No, that wasn't what I meant at all. I meant you could move in with me.'

'Move in with you?' she squeaked.

Rafe looked at her with a touch of exasperation. 'Kate, are you going to repeat absolutely everything I say?'

'Probably,' she said apologetically. 'I can't seem to think for myself right now.'

He raised one eyebrow. 'Then just sit and listen for a couple of minutes. For a start, I don't know how you'd feel about that sort of arrangement. I keep pretty irregular hours. You'd have to get used to me coming and going at all hours of the day and night. And occasionally I bring home some rather odd characters. Then there are the times I work abroad—I'd want to take you with me. How would that fit in with your plans for the future?'

'I don't really have any plans at the moment,' she admitted. 'Except for having a go at the novel, and I suppose I can do that practically anywhere. All I need is a portable typewriter and a stack of paper.'

Rafe looked at her thoughtfully. 'Then you're not totally against the idea?'

'I think I could probably get used to it,' she said, a grin beginning to spread across her face.

He seemed rather pleased. 'I didn't think it would be this easy to persuade you. I was afraid you might try to skip out of reach again.'

'Not any more.' Her grin broadened. 'You'd better get used to the idea. You've only got to crook your little finger and I'll come running,' she told him frankly, cheerfully chucking her pride right out of the window. 'When do you want me to move in with you?'

'Just as soon as we're married,' Rafe replied calmly.

Kate's eyes nearly popped out of her head. *'Married?'* she finally managed to get out in a strangled voice.

'Why are you looking so totally astounded?' enquired Rafe with some amusement. 'Hasn't the idea ever occurred to you?'

'Well—sort of,' she admitted. 'Especially since we——' She broke off and gave a rather nervous cough.

'Since we...?' prompted Rafe gently.

Kate scowled at him. 'You know perfectly well what I'm talking about!'

'Since we found out how very compatible we are?' he suggested with a sly smile.

Kate blushed bright red, and was furious with herself for getting into this totally confused state. 'I just didn't think the idea of marriage had ever occurred to *you*,' she muttered.

'It took me a couple of days to get round to the idea. But since I love you and want to live with you, it seemed like the obvious conclusion.'

And that threw Kate into a fresh welter of confusion. 'You—you love me?'

Rafe looked faintly surprised. 'I thought you knew that.'

'I don't know anything,' she retorted. 'You didn't say—you didn't tell me—I didn't know quite *what* to think,' she finished in a rather shaky voice.

His gaze settled on her reflectively. 'I thought certain things were understood between us.'

'Well, they were—but at the same time, they weren't,' she said, beginning to confuse him now, as well as herself.

Rafe gave a brief sigh. 'I'm not sure I can take much more of this. Perhaps I should just kiss you and try to convince you that way.'

'I'm not sure that's a very good idea——' she began, but he ignored her, took her into his arms, and in just seconds had reduced her to a state of complete acquiescence. He shifted closer, and his hands began to reacquaint themselves with the familiar swell of her breasts. Kate gave a faint groan, and Rafe grinned with satisfaction. Then his tongue traced the path that his fingers had taken, leaving a trail of devastation in its wake, and Kate felt as if she were melting away.

He lifted his head and took another kiss from her, this one far deeper and more demanding than the last. Then he seemed to realise that things were running away from them, because he released her again rather quickly, and then pushed her away from him.

'Damn it, Kate,' he said rather shakenly. 'I think you'd better stay away from me for a couple of minutes, or this is all going to get completely out of control!'

She grinned weakly back at him. 'It's all your fault. You shouldn't have so much of the Clarendon charm. You know what it does to females!'

'You're the only female I'm interested in right now,' he told her huskily. 'In fact, the only one I'm going to be interested in for the rest of my life.' He eyed her hungrily. 'Do you think we should risk one more kiss?'

'I'm not sure that we should,' Kate replied primly. 'In fact, my mother's already warned me about you. She thinks you're a bad influence on me, and that I should stay well away from you.'

'And do you always do what your mother tells you?' he growled softly.

'Not any more. So perhaps we *could* have that kiss,' she suggested, with a deliberate fluttering of her eyelashes.

It might have only been one kiss, but it seemed to go on forever. And by the time it was finally over, they were both aching for a deeper fulfilment.

Rafe moved reluctantly away from her. 'No more,' he instructed a little roughly. 'I want to wait until after we're married.'

Kate's eyebrows shot up in surprise. 'That's a pretty conventional attitude.'

'I suppose it is,' he agreed. 'But there's another way of looking at it—having to wait for something always makes it a lot better when it does finally happen.'

Kate's eyes widened. 'Better?' she said slightly breathlessly. 'Than last time?'

Rafe's gaze glittered very brightly. 'Just wait and see,' he promised in a husky tone. Then his finger traced its way down her bare arm. 'By the way,' he went on, 'don't you think there's something you should be saying to me?'

'Oh—er—yes, I suppose so,' she said, suddenly feeling ridiculously shy. She cleared her throat. 'I—I love you,' she muttered in a slightly croaky voice.

He looked at her with some amusement. 'I can't quite hear you, Kate.'

'I love you,' she repeated, in a much firmer and clearer tone.

'That's better,' he said with some satisfaction. He gave her another quick, hard kiss, and, short though it was, it actually made her knees shake. 'I don't suppose we'll have a very conventional sort of marriage,' he told her, 'but I've a feeling that it'll never be boring.'

'I certainly don't feel bored right now,' Kate whispered, sagging rather weakly against him. 'In fact, I feel . . .'

'How do you feel, Kate?' he prompted throatily. His hand returned to the curve of her breast, as if it was incapable of staying away, and Kate sighed softly as she felt a familiar heat spread over her skin.

Rafe dragged in a ragged breath. 'I think we'd better get back to England as soon as we can. I don't think I can take much more of this. A couple more days, and I'll be completely out of my mind!'

'We could catch a plane this afternoon,' she said reluctantly. 'If that's what you really want——'

'It isn't,' he said, with a grimace. 'But I'm determined to do this right. A *very* short engagement, a proper wedding with all the trimmings—and then all the time in the world to spend exactly as we please,' he murmured, his eyes glistening with anticipation.

Kate suddenly sat up very straight. 'My parents——' she said, with some trepidation. 'Once we're back in England, I'll have to tell them . . .' At the thought of breaking the news to her mother, she got increasingly flustered. 'How do you suppose they're going to take it?' she asked nervously.

'I've no idea,' Rafe replied in an unruffled tone. 'But it really makes no difference. I've no intention of changing my mind about this. I love you, Kate, and I'm going to marry you. They might not be too thrilled about it, but they won't stop it happening. And by the time we've presented them with a couple of grandchildren, even your mother might have come round to the idea.'

'Just a couple?' she teased. 'I thought half a dozen would be quite nice.'

Rafe raised one eyebrow. 'Half a dozen?'

'Well, you did like Harry,' she reminded him.

'So I did,' he said equably. 'All right, as many as you please. Although preferably not all at once!'

'Perhaps we'll stick at two or three,' she said cheerfully. Then her brows briefly drew together as a last tiny ripple of doubt suddenly surfaced. 'It will be all right, won't it?' she asked a little uncertainly. 'I mean, we've really only known each other for a short time.'

'Of course it'll be all right,' Rafe replied at once, with total assurance. 'Just trust your own feelings, Kate. They won't let you down. And neither will I.'

Kate slid her hand through his, and instantly felt calmer. It *was* going to work out perfectly, she just knew it. She and Rafe fitted together incredibly well. It was the last thing on earth that she had ever expected to happen, but, now that it had, it seemed completely right and natural. And she was absolutely certain that it would just keep getting better and better.

Rafe's grip on her hand tightened, and she gave him a happy smile. Then she sat back and began to rehearse her speech to her mother. In just a few hours, Kate was going to have to tell her that she was about to become Rafe Clarendon's mother-in-law!

 **Harlequin Presents**

is

 exotic

 dramatic

 sensual

 exciting

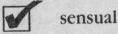 contemporary

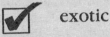 a fast, involving
read

 terrific!!

Harlequin Presents—
passionate romances
around the world!